CHAPTER 1

HER DETERMINATION TO IMPROVE

*I*t was all so awkward dealing with people.

THE MULDOON'S Home
South Dakota Prairie, 1909

Cara backed and shimmied out of a narrow space between the stacked hay bales in the pitch-black area against the barn's wall. Being on her elbows and knees were awkward enough, without adding the ordeal of her coat being two sizes too small. She was positive she heard ripping sounds where the sleeves met her shoulders. *What gave me this loopy idea to hunt the terrified creature and rescue it? Trying to get my mind off my missing little brothers — that's what.*

Wings and Storm whinnied from their stalls and Buttercup added her deep lowing.

"Hang on a minute, you two. Hey, Wings, do you have an idea of how to find our lost loves without any clues? Wish you could speak up. You might've witnessed something. Or Buttercup. Did Beth come to you for some milk to take with her? Come on, please tell me. None of us people know what happened to Beth and the boys."

Her barnyard friends said nothing.

"Nothing." At this moment, the tiny conquest she gripped in her fist must satisfy her grieving heart. If her sister, Bridget, happened by, she would receive a lecture on how she never obeys the rules about keeping the critters outside. Her newest trouble loomed with the loud squeaks emanating from it. "Shh, little thing. I've got you safe and sound. Stop squirming, and you'll see."

Something bumped her right boot sole and sniffed at her lower leg. "Blackie. Get out of my way. I can't move with you blocking me. Away Blackie." She must believe by faith that he had obeyed her as a good sheepdog ought. Her toes, rump, and arms encountered no further objects when she scrambled backward again convincing her she must be entering into the open space at last. She blew out a breath.

The little creature squirmed and squeaked while she braced her elbows on the bottom bales to stand. "I'm so thankful I wore gloves, Blackie. No telling if it's biting my fingers. Thank God in heaven."

Blackie yipped and stood on his hind legs while he pawed her arm and cocked his head.

"Hey there, boy. You're smart, so you might remember things. Did you see what happened four years ago to Beth and —"

"Cara!"

"Oh, no, it's Bridget. I was going to hide, you silly dog." Cara tucked her hands behind her back. "In here." Her sister always knew to look in the barn. It was no longer a secret place. She needed another one somewhere to do her rescuing and practice animal care. But where?

Bridget swung open the creaking doors and some scattered snowflakes drifted inside. "You're here in the dark? Are you hiding from me again? Why? What have I ever done to you to make you do that? Oh, unless it's because of the time I ordered you to help me with breakfast and you didn't want to, so you burned all the pancakes, and spilled the pail of milk, and then Da said—"

THE PERFECT CHRISTMAS FOR CARA

A COUNTRY CRITTERS & CLUES NOVELLA

THOSE RESILIENT MULDOONS

E. V. SPARROW

For my dad's family and the storytellers amongst us. To all the people who live simple, quiet, and cloistered lives who may rarely receive surprises. Merry Christmas to you.

"No, that's not it."

"Then what?" Bridget tapped her snow-clogged boot soles against the doorjamb.

"I wanted to be alone to think."

Squeaking started up from Cara's fist held behind her long wool skirt, and two of the half-grown barn cats rushed out of their own hiding places with murderous intent in their expressions. They circled her skirt. It was only a matter of time before one of them climbed it with its vicious claws. "Shoo!" This was exactly what she had wanted to avoid. Her favorite cats now turned into enemies had discovered her cute little Christmas mouse for their delightful snack, and it was her own fault. "Fiddlesticks."

Bridget stamped her foot. "Cara, have you got a mouse in your hand? I can't believe you'd capture one. Do you want it for a pet? It's a rodent. They aren't worth anything. Well, except to cats, owls, hawks—"

"I want to save it." Cara raised her fist encasing the mouse above her head. The tail hung out, but she did not plan to rearrange it now. Both young cats dug in their claws and climbed onto her swinging plaid skirt. "Bridget, help! Shoo. Tricky, off. Boo, let go." She turned quickly in a circle hoping to dislodge the predators. Without luck.

"Blackie," Bridget said, "chase."

The sheepdog hurtled toward Cara, who burst out laughing at the cats' comical expressions. Tricky and Boo's amber eyes rounded, with orange and white fur raised on their backs, tails fuzzed, and yowling to beat the wolves, they shot away from Cara's skirt and the dog's nips quick as a wink.

"Stay, Blackie. Sorry, kitties." Cara checked her fist. The mouse's tail slithered between her fingers. "Still safe." She bent and laughed so hard she held her side. "Did you see their faces, Bridget? They're so confused. Blackie is their friend. But that. I can't catch my breath."

Silence followed the boisterous event. Bridget stared down at Cara and her clenched fist with the mouse tail draped between her gloved fingers. "Hm. You care more about that mouse and the cats than your own sister, I think."

"Oh, Bridget. You know I care about you. The mouse was in here all alone with the cats, and well, someone must look out for it. Don't you see? It's at the mercy of nature. A piece of food. Helpless. Unaware of what lurks around it ready to snatch it away." Her throat constricted and more words stuck like a clogged drain in the kitchen sink.

"Little sister." Bridget sniffed. "You're such a softy for the creatures, but it sounds more like you're speaking of our youngest brothers. Aren't you? You still awaken me with your nightmares. I've bad dreams as well."

Cara sniffed. So many unanswered questions about Finn and Callum's disappearance with their mother, Beth, and the terrible fears for them she could not express around their father. She gulped down a stone of sadness. "I'm afraid to speak of them because Da blames himself. What can be done to find them? We need some clues."

Bridget slowly shook her head. "I don't know what else can be done. But if anyone can find clues and all of them, you know Liam will. Our brilliant brother is so stubborn and brave. He said he's looking for them and won't ever give up. We must count on that. We can pray every day, as well. I do. Do you? Maybe —"

"Girlies! *Macushlas*. Are you inside with the cats? Aye?" Boots crunched loudly in the snow between the clapboard house, built by the *Chicago, Milwaukee & St. Paul Railway*, and the barn.

"Quick, Cara. Go into the shadows. I'll make an excuse for you, but you must hide the Christmas mouse. Hurry. Then return to help me with supper." Bridget rushed to the barn doors and stopped. "Oh, dear. Supper was on the stove. On my way, Da."

Time to plan for where to keep the mouse and what to safely put it in. Cara surveyed the stall housing Wings. He nuzzled her arm. "You need your supper. I know."

The pail might do. She removed it from its nail on the wall and gingerly released the tiny gray mouse. It scampered in circles — scraping its little claws against the metal. "Hey. Your name is Scampers."

Wings threw his head and twitched his ears forward. Cara allowed

4

him to snuffle at the pail. "No worries. I'll get the other one." She collected another pail hanging on the rail of the indoor pen where Da housed the sheep for the winter. They bleated their fears and shoved each other to the far side of the enclosure. "Why you're all scaredy cats after knowing me for years completely puzzles me. Don't you recognize the person that takes care of you? Silly creatures. I've never hurt one strand of wool on any of you."

The horses shuffled in their impatience. "Hold on. Getting your grain." Cara set the mouse pail inside the sheep's pen knowing the cats dared not go near the excitable white fuzzy animals. She quickly dipped the empty pail into the burlap sack of oats and carried them to Wings' stall. The Percheron must be the hungriest. After she satisfied his hunger with oats and hay, and fed Storm, the cow, and the sheep, she scanned the dim barn again.

Tricky and Boo slunk around the bales with their heads low in search of Scampers.

The cats were onto her and knew their snack was nearby. What to do with the mouse and the pail? Think. The house would not be safe, would it? Maybe she could try that. She could put Scampers in one of her bureau's drawers. There must be a box or something in a closet.

"Cara girlie."

She startled, her heart pounding, and twisted around. "Da?"

He stood in the orange light of the setting sun behind him. "You're needed in the kitchen. Bridget is beside herself with tears. You know I'm no good at dealing with that, aye? Make haste."

"Yes, Da. I'm finishing up with Storm and will be there soon. All right?" She smiled and hoped he would accept her promise so she could hide Scampers somehow.

He waved his thick gloved hand above his head. "Aye. Then come see to your sister. Blackie, boy-o, with me."

Cara paused until his crunching footsteps faded, then rushed to the pen, alarming the sheep, the cats, and Storm. She snatched up the pail. After she reached in and carefully clamped onto Scampers, she stuffed her hand inside her tight coat. The rips. She must see to those tonight. But first the mouse and her sister. Why could she not stay in the barn with the animals forever and hide from people? It was all so awkward dealing with people.

***

Icy air blew into Cara's face when she stepped through the barn doors. She shivered and paused while she tugged her scarf up over her lower face with her empty hand. It took a moment being hindered by her wobbly gloves. No hand-me-downs ever fit her. Is that smoke? As Cara drew nearer to the house, the stench grew. "Oh no. Poor Bridget." She hurried to the porch and tugged open the door. A small cloud of smoke escaped past her.

"I'm beside myself, Da. When Cara finally gets here, maybe she can help me figure out what to do for supper. That girl is always too busy with her animals to have a care for what I do for us plus she hides when I need her. Why she can't do both, I'm sure I don't know. Our Moira did everything when she was Cara's age. Your Beth took care of the household chores and the boys and the —"

"And now she's gone with the boys, me Bridget. No one ever took care of her, aye?"

"Oh, Da. Didn't mean to bring that up. Here I am complaining too much, aren't I?"

Cara stomped her boots in the entry area. I'm in more trouble now. Forgot to do that on the porch. "I'm here. Sorry Bridget. I'll clean up the snow on the floor."

Bridget and their father stood inside the kitchen scowling at her. Another reason she liked being alone. It was uncomfortable never pleasing anyone.

"I almost gave up hope for your help with supper, Cara. What did you do out there? Build a snow fort? Put up a Christmas tree? Deliver our jars of blackberry jam to all the neighbors?" Bridget sniffed and brushed away tears from her pink cheeks.

She has the most beautiful skin. No freckles. Unfair.

Scampers squirmed in her glove.

Good heavens. I'm always upsetting my sister. Cara flushed and huffed out a breath. How much time had passed? "Did the chores.

That's all. I'll be right back. I promise." She turned toward the hall to rush off to the bedroom and stash Scampers somewhere.

Her father boomed, "Cara, girlie. What's happened to your coat? The sleeves are torn asunder in the back. Are you wounded? Was there a mishap?"

"No, Da. I am well. Be back in a minute." She hurried down the hallway, tracking more melting snow.

Bridget's shrieks about ill treatment echoed down the hall to Cara's bedroom.

"I've poked the bear this time, haven't I?" She slid open the bottom bureau drawer. Mostly empty. Gingerly, she opened her gloved fist, and Scampers popped out onto an old woolen scarf unused since Cara's mother left several years ago. It was not easy to part with some of her mother's clothing. "Poor Da. Two wives have left him."

"Of course you're hiding in your bedroom. Why else would you be crouching down there between your bed and the bureau?" Bridget gripped her hips. If she was a dog, she'd be snarling.

Cara stood and shoved the drawer closed with her boot. "I need dry socks." Spying a tear rolling down Bridget's cheek, Cara bit her lip. "I'll follow you now. Really." What aid she could offer her sister in the kitchen must be a secret easy to keep, for she didn't know. "Tell me what to do, sister."

Bridget turned her back on Cara and stomped her way out to the kitchen. "Do you think I can teach you to cook in one night? I only had to because Moira and Beth made me. Being two years older than you, and you didn't wish to learn it when you had the chance." She suddenly stopped and Cara plowed into her. "You no longer have a choice. Why only the other day at the mercantile when I ran into Sally, I had to invent a story as to why you weren't shopping with me. It's not easy being your older sister, you know. How am I supposed to explain to curious folks that you're not interested in womanly chores but only in —"

"Bridget." Mick stood from the bench where he'd tugged on his boots, then dawned his remaining outdoor clothing of wool hat, and gloves. "Holy heavens. Leave your sister be, aye? There's supper to get.

The darkness is setting in, and we must be up at dawn. Fix us morsels that're quick. Whilst I wait, I shall be away to the barn to check on how much room is left for wintering the livestock." He grabbed a lantern and called over his shoulder before he shut the door against drifting snowflakes. "One of you may fetch me when food is on the table."

"My boots, Bridget." Cara sat on the wooden bench still warm from her father. She pulled off the one size too big clunkers. They kept her feet warm enough with three pairs of layered socks. But wouldn't it be lovely to have one piece of clothing fit her? It was always the leftovers for herself. The baby of the family now. She didn't want to be the baby. Yet, how terrible it would be without the leftovers. She perked up. "I shall be happy to have them."

"And I shall be happy to have you in the kitchen. What are you mumbling about?" Bridget stood in the pantry digging around inside.

"About how sad life would be without leftovers. I wish I wasn't the baby, but I'm determined to be happy that people give me their unwanted or ill-fitting clothing. At least it keeps me from becoming a human icicle. How about pancakes and eggs for dinner, Bridget? It's the only thing I know how to cook."

"Plus, it's fast like Da requested." Bridget backed out of the closet of foodstuffs cradling the flour and clenching the basket's handle of eggs nestled inside. "Like-minded, aren't we?" Her sweet smile reassured Cara the storm between them had passed.

Cara took the basket of eggs from Bridget and set them on the counter by the wood stove.

Bridget checked the stove's fire. "You can beat the eggs, and I'll measure in the milk and flour."

"That's jolly." Cara cracked the eggs into the large white bowl they always used for pancake batter. She peeked up at her sister. "I'm determined to use Christmas words as much as possible. I don't like it when we fight. We only have each other at home now. Don't you think we should try to be close and love each other no matter what?"

Bridget smirked. "Deck the halls with love? Yeah, you mean no matter how badly you behave or how much you forget things or how mad I get when —"

"Yes. All of that. Please?" Cara grinned as wide as possible, hoping her charming dimples showed.

"Of course." Her sister kissed the top of her head. "We will always love each other. Let's hurry, then you can fetch Da. Wear my coat until we can mend yours. See? I can be as good as Moira."

Cara shook her head. "My determination is that I'll try to be like her as well. Although, no one is as good as Moira. Hark, the herald angels sing. God, may You bless her angelic soul."

***

CHAPTER 2

HER WILLPOWER WAVERS

ne Week Later

"Mimicking Moira the angel will never work." Nor imitating that flibbertigibbet Bridget. "I loathe cooking, cleaning, and doing the laundry. I'd rather be here with you, Wings. Sewing or mending hurts my eyes, and embroidery is not a creative endeavor like drawing. Bah! Bridget will say anything is creative to get my cooperation. Look at my poor fingertips. Poked to pieces. Fingers are not supposed to resemble Beth's pin cushion, are they?"

Wings chewed his grain. He did not worry about what humans did other than feed him on time and ride him every day. She would return and do that after a while. If the snow held off.

Their cow lowed for Cara's attention. "Hey Buttercup, girl. Yeah, it's your turn. How did you sleep? You do much better with giving us milk if you're all relaxed, right?" Cara situated the low stool and the empty pail stored in the cow's stall. "How about a Christmas carol? Let's see. *Away In a Manger* will do."

The hens stopped clucking for a moment after her first stanza. Buttercup turned her head to stare at her and stopped chewing. Embarrassment flooded through Cara, and she stopped singing.

"What? I'm told my voice is nice." She shifted on the stool for better balance and continued the pattern of the song to match her milk streams pinging against the metal pail's wall. "Now this is very creative. I dare you to do this, grumpy older sister."

Tricky and Boo meowed for their warm breakfast and rubbed against Cara's legs as she sang. She gave them a few squirts, which spread milk over their faces. The cats closed their eyes and licked at the airborne streams. *Glad they don't know about Scampers in my pocket.*

"Hilarious."

Cara sent a squirt of milk up Buttercup's belly and into her own face. "Josie Halloway. Are you spying on me?" *She was a most unwelcome guest.*

"My father is visiting your father. I can't think of a good reason for it." Josie scrunched up her pretty upturned nose.

Wiping her damp face with her coat sleeve, Cara glanced away from her enemy. Of course Josie would wear a stylish red, girlish coat her rich dad got for her. *I can't wear red. And girlish isn't me either.* Josie's fancy boots weren't someone's castoffs.

"Daddy has mostly influential friends. What do you think?"

Cara ground her teeth. *If only she were Buttercup, and she could stomp on that smug, sneaky snake.* "I can't guess why he'd come here either." She stared at her enemy's fancy clad feet while continuing her milking. "Or why you'd come inside the barn in those boots."

Josie peered down at her feet and tipped them slightly for inspection. "Oh. I don't own your type of boots. Work boots, I mean. We have maids and farmhands to do chores at our home. Grandmother would never let me wear anything but the best, of course. She's a staunch believer in the more refined aspects of living. Wasn't your mother or grandmother like that as well?"

Spoiled cat. Cara scowled and turned her focus back to her task. *She knows full well the story of Ma and Beth.* "I'm surprised you're up early. It's still dark. Only farmers and ranchers need to be out working hard before sunup. They're heroes feeding their families and the entire world." *I may not be angelic like Moira, but I am telling God's truth.*

"Hm. I suppose so." Josie snuffled the air, then let out a dainty cough. "I just do not know how you can stand the smell in here. Does it bother you? Oh my. How impolite of me to say that aloud. You must not notice the stench by now."

Cara scooted the stool far enough away from Buttercup's belly to stand and face Josie with clenched fists. "You're a —"

"Well, now, young ladies. Isn't it grand to see you girls together?" Mick Muldoon led Josie's father into the barn filled with tension. If her father were an animal, he would be an oblivious puppy. "We were saying how we'd enjoy seeing the friendship between you. Aye, Mr. Holloway?"

"Yes, yes. Josie has many friends, don't you, pet? Did you invite your friend to your Christmas party?" Holloway turned to Mick. "She pressed me through late last night to bring her here with me until I gave in, for she determined to speak to your daughter about it. Such a kind heart she has."

Nausea swirled in Cara's tummy. She tucked in her lips to keep from responding. *He means his most detestable daughter's cruel heart. She no doubt wanted to gloat — not invite me.*

Josie cuddled against her father's arm and gave Cara and Mick a syrupy smile. "I was about to tell her, Daddy, but you interrupted. Please, Cara, come to my party next Friday? It is three days before Christmas. We made certain to choose a night not too close to any Christmas Eve celebrations." She batted her long black lashes at her dear daddy. "Absolutely everyone and anyone is invited. It is the season for charity, is it not?" She slowly scanned the barn. "Especially for those who need it."

Blackie plopped on Cara's feet. He seemed to know what kind of human that girl was. "I might. I don't know. There's always much to do here —"

"Cara, girlie. You can skip your chores this once, and I shall do them, aye?" Her own father betrayed her! She knew what that sparkle in his blue eyes meant. But why would he challenge her on this? She could not care less about an uppity party with snooty people.

"I must check Bridget's plans first, don't you think, Da?"

Josie gasped. "Oh. The invitation is also for your sister Bridget. Did I forget to say? It is of no matter that she is a teeny bit older. I am also older than you, dear Cara. Age is not an issue." She coughed and clutched her throat. "Daddy, I think the hay and — you know what else — is bothering me. Can we leave now?"

Mr. Holloway removed his gold timepiece from his pocket. "My, my, we ought to catch our train soon. Josie's grandmother complains for days if we are not punctual. It will be a busy day and a long trip to the city."

Cara frowned. To have a grandmother. How lovely and fun that would be.

"Oh, Daddy. It is only because she makes such wonderful plans and fills up the days with so many outings that we cannot attend everything if we are late." She curtsied to Mick. "Thank you for your hospitality, Mr. Muldoon. It is very, um, interesting here."

"Aye, young lady. 'Tis at that." Mick swung a quick glance at Cara and gave a shake of his head before he extended his hand. "Mr. Holloway. 'Twas me pleasure doing business with you."

Mr. Holloway guffawed. "I am sure we will be doing more business in the future, for you have seen my jumbled skills at cards." He draped his arm over Josie's shoulders and headed for the doors.

Josie peeked back at Cara over her father's arm, for she was tall like Bridget. Cara caught the malice in her green eyes and wondered what game she was playing. Absolutely nothing Cara would enjoy. Josie's sneaky games were always about causing misery for others.

That was another reason she liked animals better than people. Except for Jesus, who was nice and good. Wise and kind as well. But He was unusual. She hummed *Away In a Manger* again and took a step toward Buttercup. "Poor thing. I'm neglecting you because of that mean old cat —"

"Cara?"

She skipped a step and twisted around. "You're still here, Da?"

13

He chuckled. "And you're away with the fairies. I take it you two girlies don't like each other at all?"

"As you would say — not one whit." Cara shooed Tricky and Boo away from the pail and straightened the stool. She sat and leaned against Buttercup to finish the milking and spoke over her shoulder. "I am resolved to be more like Moira, yet it's impossible. You don't know Josie like I do. She can fool her father, but not the rest of us at school."

Mick leaned against the stall to face his youngest daughter. He crossed his arms and studied her. "She can't fool everyone, macushla. I took her measure quick as a blink. You know her mother passed when she was young? Makes a bit of difference, aye? Losing your own ma should give you some understanding of Josie. Nothing replaces a mother's love. Even a father's cannot. 'Tis not quite the same."

Cara sighed and scrunched her shoulders to shove off the guilt pressing down on her. "Da, please don't make me feel bad. She's the one who says and does mean things. I don't want to feel any empathy for her."

"Honesty is a grand thing to help us switch to another path. Give it some thought, aye? Me time ran out with both your mother and Beth before I could change and stop drinking the cursed whiskey. 'Twas a terrible thing with many misfortunate losses, macushla." He kicked a wheelbarrow's tire beside him.

"I'll think about what you've said." One day.

Mick shoved away from the stall and slid his gloved hands inside his coat. "I don't work on the rails today, so I'll be moving the chickens and building an indoor coop. 'Tis leaning terribly since that last blizzard passed through. Shall you wish to assist your father?"

"You know me. Anything to avoid housework. Maybe that's one of Mr. Holloway's problems. He doesn't really know anything about his own daughter." She pushed Tricky away from her leg. "Her claws get me every time."

"Aye could be. Nonetheless, you shouldn't speak 'bout Josie as a cat."

14

Cara giggled. "Was talking about Tricky in her eagerness for the milk. I imagine Josie as a snake. Or a cat with claws as well."

Mick scowled. "If you think of people critically, there'll come a day when you speak your thoughts aloud, and you can't undo the damage."

"Fine." Cara stood. She lifted the full pail away from the cats' reach and caused their outrage. "Down kitties. You've had your breakfast. Da, why did Mr. Holloway even come here? He never has."

Mick grasped the heavy milk pail from her. "I wish to say you don't need to know, but I'll tell you. He lost a sum of money to me in a card game down at the saloon." He waggled his graying brows. "Aye, 'tis a helpful thing for Christmas gifts. 'Tis all I'll share for we ought to get inside to tell Bridget we've not deserted her."

"Right. We've wounds from desertions." Her father spoke of his whiskey drinking and the consequences. She followed him and chewed her lip. Her gloves grew hot inside from the sweat building on her palms. Dare I ask?

Blackie met them at the doors, and Mick held one open for her. "You're yet troubled, me girlie?"

She faced him. "Da, when you go to the saloon to play cards, do you drink?" She held a breath.

"Not often nor as much, Cara." He surveyed the swollen clouds above them, and spread wide over the prairie, then shut the heavy door. Scooting the heavy rock in front of the one that would sometimes swing open in the wind, he shifted the full pail. "Not to worry. Me drinking days are done, and by me own choice. Thinking 'tis why I win more often at the cards." He winked, then limped with his usual and painful gait alongside her.

Cara slowly released her breath. "Thank you for saying so, Da." His strong need for whiskey had caused the family so much harm. Seen enough of that to never, ever touch alcohol. She headed to the house with him and up the porch steps.

Bridget swung open the door the exact moment Cara reached for the handle. "I've been watching you two from the kitchen window. What were you doing for so long? The eggs and toast are cold along with the coffee." She threw her flour sack towel through the doorway into the kitchen. "You can reheat it for yourselves. I'm going to my room to lie down."

"Sister, don't be upset. We're happy to feed ourselves." Cara stepped forward to follow her.

"No, macushla. Leave her be a moment." Mick raised his brows. "Bridget's been touchy of late, and she must have suitable reasons for it. Let's fetch our meal as she said. Then you may be a good sister and go to her." He lifted the milk pail onto the counter.

It took Cara a short time to reheat the lukewarm food on their plates. "If I could prepare meals by warming up already cooked food, I'd certainly do it. My abilities wouldn't mess it up. Here's your plate and coffee, Da. I'm leaving Bridget's until she comes back. Twice-warmed food wouldn't be tasty, and especially in her offended state of mind."

"Aye, you're a clever one. I'll say the blessing. Bless us O Lord, for these Thy gifts, for which we are 'bout to receive through Christ our Lord, Amen."

They made the sign of the cross, then ate in silence as Mick had taught his family. Conversation always waited until after they emptied their plates.

Cara scraped up the last of her eggs, and Mick sopped up the yolk left on his plate with his toast. He dropped a piece of crust for Blackie waiting beneath his chair and laid his fork down. "Let's be sure to thank her for her efforts."

"Da, I'm worried about Bridget. Aren't you? She used to be happy and sing, and laugh at the oddest things, but lately, she's not herself. What can I do?" Cara gathered their dishes and utensils to set into the sink. "It can't be about Beth and our missing brothers because it's been four years since."

Mick leaned back in his chair and ran his hands through his wavy, gray hair. "Time drags on whilst we search for our macushlas. Holidays are when we feel it the keenest, aye?" He slid his chair back and motioned to Blackie.

Cara wiped her moist cheek and nose. "I desperately need Moira's advice. She's been gone for six years, and we've only seen her three times. Has she written to say she can get away from her duties at the convent and come home for Christmas? That would cheer Bridget and me more than anything."

Her father stepped close to her and stroked her frizzy head. "You're on your way to an adult now, aye, and many a duty binds us adults. Nonetheless, some are most enjoyable. You must find those and add them into your life. Moira found hers." He kissed her forehead. "Join me at the barn after you speak to your sister. The weather should hold fair."

Cara twisted around to stare down the shadowy hallway to the bedrooms. *I'd rather be with the chickens. They're simply happy when I throw seed at them.*

***

CHAPTER 3

HER SISTERLY DEVOTION

*T*he Following Day

Cara and Bridget awoke to the rooster's crow as they did every early morning. The sisters staying up into the wee hours chatting did not affect their rooster, clock or the sunrise. She stretched and yawned. Bridget did not budge. "That girl can sleep through anything. I envy her."

"I heard that. I'm trying to ignore the morning. Can't we sleep until it's light out for once?" Bridget turned over to face Cara. "It was like old times with Moira last night. Hiding under the quilt. Talking about our lives and dreaming about the future. She would have said a prayer for us, though. We forgot — I don't know why. Must she be with us to pray? We're quite grown enough not to need her suggestions. But let's make hot chocolate next time, so I must get us some. Remember the first time we gathered for a meeting when she had us all sitting on the kitchen floor by the stove and Liam was there, too, and —"

"Bridget!" Mick's shout startled both his daughters. "Where are you, girlie?"

Cara flapped the quilt back and shivered. "We're together, Da. One moment." She slid her feet into her slippers and removed Scampers from the bureau drawer. "Hey, Sis, I'll stoke the coals in the stove to give you some more rest. Like we spoke about last night. Moira always said we should count on each other for everything we can, and I've already resolved to be more like her. Failing so far, aren't I?"

Bridget hugged the quilt and scooted up against her pillow. "You? I'm mortified by my own selfishness. All I've done is complain about the workload. Do you think Da wishes he still had Moira? I know he wishes —"

"Bridget." Cara paused at the closed door. "I feel a long chat brewing for tonight, don't you? Let's get to the chores. I made Buttercup wait entirely too long yesterday. She's bound to refuse to give us milk this time. I would if I were her. Fingers crossed she's not like me."

"You're always making comparisons between animals and people. It doesn't work that way, silly." Bridget shuffled into the hallway behind Cara.

"What? I'm not the silly one — you are. I can't believe you called me that."

"Why not? It's true. I think you compared me to a llama once. You've never even been around one in your entire life."

Cara scoffed. "I saw one in a book at school. I'll show it to you since you only like books with pictures in them."

"I read fine, thank you. You're the one who likes pictures because you're an artist. Or you used to be. Whatever happened to your —"

"Bridget, you're no fun to argue with because of your rabbit trails."

"Good afternoon, *macushlas*." They had arrived in the kitchen, where Mick sat with his empty coffee cup and an empty plate. "'Tis glad I am to see you're both well and sniping at each other again." He wrecked his scold with a dimpled grin. "One can always count on the Muldoon girlies to bicker and yammer at each other whilst the chores wait until evening, aye?"

"Oh, Da." Cara's face flushed. She'd failed again to treat Bridget with sisterly love. Would she ever get it right? "My apologies. I'm to blame for our tardiness." She elbowed her sister. "We'll hurry to catch up." She opened the stove's door to stoke the coals and found kindling already added and fueling the fire.

"You did this, Da?"

Mick frowned. "Not I — the Fairies must've been here. Or mayhap our little house Brownies grew cold in the wee hours. One can never tell how quick and strong they are."

Bridget giggled. "Thank you for helping me this morning, Da." She enfolded his head and shoulders in a quick squeeze from behind.

"Now, now. Get away with you. 'Twas no trouble. Nonetheless, can you be hastily getting to the breakfast? The day isn't waiting for Mick Muldoon to begin it. I'm due at the tracks and directing the crew. Cara, your creatures await you in the barn. You'll be eating after them."

Cara grimaced in defeat at Bridget, who shrugged in return. "On my way." Her tummy growled. An important rule of animal husbandry — minister to your critters' needs first.

***

A shadow blocked the sunbeam across the heap of hay Cara forked for Buttercup. Her heart thumped. She turned toward whatever it was. "Hallo, Sis. Almost done."

Bridget carried a cup of steaming coffee and extended it. "Thank you for taking the blame for our late meal. This is my amends from your grumpy older sister for my part in that. Don't you get worn out from your chores sometimes? I do. Why only last Wednesday while —"

"Maybe I don't work as hard." Cara breathed in the liquid's pungent aroma, closed her eyes, and took a sip. "Ah. A morning without coffee is still night. If we're not careful, we'll become a happy family. All this caring for one another. Think it'll last?"

Tricky and Boo meowed at Cara's legs and tried to grab the full milk bucket from her grip. "Hey, kitties. You did this yesterday and the day before, yet you may still not have second breakfasts."

Bridget giggled. "Let me take it. They can't reach it if I hold it, can they? I'm almost a foot taller than you."

Cara handed the bucket over. "Are you saying I'm too short? I don't need to be told about it. Mighty things can be tiny, you know."

"Like a stick of dynamite? That's what I'll start calling you — Cara-mite."

"Don't you dare call me that."

Bridget smacked her forehead. "I forgot. I came in to tell you that your breakfast is cold. Cara-mite." She whipped around, nearly sloshing the milk out of the bucket, stepped on Boo's tail — the kitty yowled and dashed away, and Bridget hurried outside. "Sorry, Boo!"

With the chores being done, and her cup empty, Cara rushed after her sister. Her breath puffed around her like a smokestack. Their father was at work, and since it was a Saturday, they should make some fun plans. No chores. What had he said to her last night? "Some duties are enjoyable, and I must find those to add to my life."

What duties or tasks did she like to do? Ride Wings, play with animals, draw, create things, and read. *Reading is at school, and I already take care of the animals. I'll talk to my huge sister for ideas. Maybe she can see things better from her great height.* She grinned. "Mount Bridget."

Blackie greeted her inside the door with a tail wag. His winter job while the livestock was protected indoors was keeping guard at the door, alarming the family to visitors or trespassers, and enjoying a needed rest.

"Forgot to take you with me, sweet boy, in my rush to get the chores done. Promise we'll go later."

Bridget turned away from the stove when Cara sat at the table and Blackie laid beneath it. "I've got your warm plate. Look at how good we're doing at getting along today." She untied her yellow apron and took a chair while her sister dug into her breakfast.

"Thank you for heating it up." Cara mumbled with her mouth full.

"Moira would be so proud of us. Or she might not believe how we're getting along. Want some milk? You worked for it." Bridget rose and ladled it into Cara's cup. "When I think of all our spats that she had to deal with for all those years of our childhood, it makes my face burn with shame. Remember the time —"

Cara raised her hand. "No spat recollections, please. But I'm sorry for being a childish younger sister. We're fifteen and seventeen now, so we can start over, right?"

"You mean nearly sixteen and eighteen but agreed." Bridget leaned forward on her elbows. "What should we do? There's dusting, sweeping, mopping, oh, and sorting through all the things we don't use. Do you know how dusty it —"

"Something, enjoyable for today. Not chores." Cara set her fork on her plate with a clink.

"It's two weeks to Christmas Eve, and we should make our home festive, don't you think? I'd love to improve the mood in our home since we're resolving to change ourselves."

Bridget folded her arms and sulked. "That's all fine for you. Your chores are done. Mine aren't."

Blackie scrambled out from under the table with Bridget's shrill tone.

"This isn't fair. If we do your idea, I'll have to make up the time for skipping my work. Really, Cara-mite, you haven't grown up that —"

"Stop complaining, Mount Bridget. I'd help you to do your work as well. Let's make a goal to do all of it by supper time. I'll even cook with you. Agreed?" Cara folded her hands like a prayer and raised her brow.

Bridget stood and stared down at her sister. "First, you called me Mount Bridget. You meant it to mock me, but I like that nickname. Shirley Moore says that she wishes she were as tall as —"

"I wish it as well. Can we keep trying to cooperate with each other today?" She raised crossed fingers. "I promise to help you do one chore if you promise to help me with one task. That's fair, right?"

"Hm." Bridget paced the area between the stove and the back door with Blackie following her back and forth. He must be bored with his silly humans and wants some excitement. She stopped to stare out the kitchen window overlooking the barn and paddock. "Only one chore?"

Cara shrugged. "More if we have time. I'm choosing to help you sort through stuff because you told me your list. The only thing I want help with is to gather some greenery to decorate for Christmas. It's a fun activity to me. What do you think?"

"Well, it is a fine day out. Cold as yesterday probably. But so will it be tomorrow —"

"Mount Bridget. Hurry up and say yes, for heaven's sake." Cara stroked the dog's back as he trod past her chair. "We're taking Blackie out with us. Poor thing needs some exercise, and the snow is shallow."

"Let's go. But only because you promised to help me sort the junk."

They bundled up against the frigid air with coats, scarves, gloves and hats. Bridget had mended Cara's coat as well as her skill allowed, but the draft came through. Cara shuddered yet ignored it with willpower.

Bridget carried the basket they used to collect their chicken's eggs, and Cara tacked up Wings. She was itching for a ride although it was a short distance to the creek. That's where they would find the best trees and shrubs for their greenery. Cara kneed Wings forward. Eagerness for a ride sparked her spirit — as her father had said adding things she likes to her life would be.

"If we find too much to carry, Cara, you should return for Wings' cart. That might be overly optimistic, but maybe not. It's been a mild winter so far, and Sara Thompson said the almanac predicts —"

"Hurry, Mount Bridget." Cara urged Wings into a canter. "We're going on ahead. Meet you there."

"Why are you in such a rush? Sis!"

Cara leaned forward over Wings' withers and breathed in deep of the crisp air forcing its way through the scarf wrapped over her face. Riding is freedom. Tension blows away. Any amount of time in nature infused hope into her spirit. *I don't know why it does.*

They rounded the bend and headed down the shallow incline toward the massive boulder marking the creek and small frozen pond. Bridget's prediction was not true. The shrubs had leaves, which must be enough. Many bushes lined the bank, but the trees had lost their leaves. Branches could suit. "A few have mistletoe, Wings. Although, they're a little too high for me."

Cara slowed Wings to a walk and reined him in beneath the largest tree a short distance from the boulder. If only they were close together. How could she reach the mistletoe patch? She was brilliant to not stand on Wings' back — which probably wouldn't take her high enough anyway.

A train whistle blew in the distance. She shaded her eyes from the winter sun's glare from above and scanned the stark, white rolling hills surrounding the railroad town for miles. It had sprung up when they built the tracks and needed supplies for the crews. The town, train, and a smatter of trees were the only color to break the rise and fall of the vast whiteness. A trail of steam dissipated as the train's speed increased. "Yep, there it goes to the next stop. Wonder how Da is doing out there?" Liam was much further down the track in another town.

Footsteps crunched and slid in the crusty snow behind Cara. "My goodness. Doesn't that whistle take you back to the day Moira left us for the convent? I'm still a little vexed about it. Why did she want to be a nun? I never understood that, but don't tell her I said so. I know that you or I never would be nuns. Can you imagine how —"

"You may be right, but Da said that's what she added to her life to make her spirit happy." Cara stomped her feet, hugged herself against the chill, and turned around to her sister. She stooped to stroke Blackie. "Da told me that yesterday. I chose Christmas decorations, and she chose helping God. Doesn't compare, does it? Even so, we all can choose whatever we want to do according to what's in our hearts."

Bridget swung her arms and clapped her hands. "Well, my heart chooses inside things. Like vaudeville or singing at church or sewing or — oh my. Do you see something moving toward us on the hill?"

"No. Which hill?" Cara squinted hard.

Blackie stepped forward, ears alert, as did Wings. They both stared and listened.

A howl echoed from nearby and Blackie growled with Wings

throwing his head and sidestepping. Cara snatched his reins. "Bridget, grab a big branch."

"What in the world is a wolf or coyote doing prowling around us during the day? Aren't they supposed to hunt at night?" Her voice shook.

"They've adapted and they're still hungry. Stay, Blackie." Cara held Wings' reins tightly. "Oh no. Did I shut the barn doors? Quick, get the branch. We must run back!"

Bridget broke off a branch with some valiant effort, and they all rushed to the incline giving them a clear view of the barn. The doors were shut.

"I did remember. Thank you, God." Cara stood beside her sister, and monitored Blackie and Wings, who swung their heads and peered around without further signs of fear. What should they do? "Do you want to go inside, Sis?"

Bridget bit her lip and slid a wide glance at her sister. "Our choice is staying here with a big branch or going closer to the barn where the wolf might be? Not a chance. I'm sticking close to all of you and wishing I'd never left the house."

Cara released a pent-up breath and motioned to Blackie to keep alert on the hill. "Let's gather what we can and get home. Wings seems recovered. I'll get a branch and be watchful."

"I wish I was as brave as you, Cara-mite, but I've got the shudders. I never expected a wolf or a coyote." She clutched her throat and stared wide-eyed around the hills.

The sisters broke off several branches of shrubs while they monitored Blackie on the hill. After they filled the basket, and the threat did not return, they relaxed. Cara sang her favorite Christmas song, *Away In a Manger*, and Bridget joined in with her clear, lilting soprano.

Cara shivered. "This coat is allowing the cold inside, so it's messing up my enjoyment. Are you done?" She'd forgotten to face the hill, as did Bridget.

Blackie barked frantically — Cara's heart jumped in her chest, and Bridget dropped her basket of greenery.

The girls shrieked and grabbed their long branches from off the ground.

A tall woman's form stood atop the hill where the dog now sat, happy as a butterfly. "Well, now. Isn't this a familiar thing? Many a year has passed us by, nevertheless, me memory of this pond and the brouhaha remains forever etched into it."

"Auntie Orla!" The girls chimed together and scurried up the hill.

***

CHAPTER 4

HER ONLY AUNTIE

"Aye, me young ladies. Secretly planned to come bearing gifts to delight you. Meaning I didn't warn your Da." The purple feathers on her hat twisted in the wind like a tornado, and her rose perfume stirred up envy for the flower bush. "What are you two girlies up to? You're not ensnaring me to go to the pond. I'll pay neither for new boots nor dresses this time. Let's have a hot brandy instead."

Cara and Bridget giggled together.

Bridget hugged her Auntie Orla again. "You can't shock us. We know you don't drink, Auntie O. You told us that on every one of your visits, trying to shame our father into giving up his whiskey."

Orla raised a brow. "Don't I know it? Coffee shall do the trick."

The sisters quickly collected up nature's bounty, and what Bridget had turned over from the basket onto the snow. They slid on some hidden ice and knocked into each other with both landing on their rumps. When their laughter ceased, they gathered up their pickings with their auntie's help.

"Isn't it good to laugh? Although you may not think that right now, sister with the sore backside." Cara climbed the base of the boulder and mounted Wings, then called Blackie to stay with her women.

"Auntie O, did you see a wolf or a coyote sniffing around as you approached our home?"

"That I didn't. The sleigh driver encountered nothing odd on our ride up from the station. When you weren't inside, I left me bags and followed your tracks, which told me where to find you down the hill. No surprises for me at all. Nevertheless, I can smite a wolf on me own, aye?"

"That's reassuring. I'll meet you back at the house after I get Wings settled." Cara urged her horse toward home. Along the way, she scanned the trail marks in the snow, and sure enough, she found two sets of dog prints. Blackie hadn't gone back and forth. Her heart pounded. Thank God's goodness we'd moved the chickens indoors with the sheep.

Glad she'd also shut and locked the doors — she rode around the barn's exterior to check where the predator had sniffed around. It had circled it, then its paw prints disappeared down the knoll heading west. Only one hungry creature — not a pack. That's a relief.

Unease swirled through Cara's imagination. Predators hadn't taken away Beth and the boys, had they? Hunters had been ridding the prairie of wolves for a few years now. Surely, they wouldn't attack an adult woman with two small children. It couldn't be true. Cara shook her head forcefully to erase the horrific image. "Silly Cara Muldoon, don't allow wild imaginations to destroy the joy in today."

The chickens clucked, and the sheep were baaing as an alarm to Cara of their near catastrophe. Wings shook his white mane. "Don't worry, everyone, I'll tell Da and keep on the watch for the critter." For now, it was time to settle Wings and get on with the day's festivities.

After she brushed and settled the horse, she checked her skirt pocket for Scampers. The squirmy lump reassured her he was there, but she must sneak the mouse back into the drawer before her aunt discovers it and the little guy frightens her into fits.

Shrieks of laughter carried through the front door when Cara opened it after stomping the snow from her work boots. Blackie rose from his spot, blocking the doorway, and licked her gloved hand. "Hold on, you two. I'm already missing the jolliness."

Bridget peeked through the kitchen entry. "We're only now starting. Hurry! Auntie O reminded me of the pond incident when we hunted for tadpoles."

"Oh, I remember that well. You told her I shoved you into the water and ruined your boots to trick her into getting you a new pair." Cara removed her own boots and slid her feet into her slippers by the bench under the hat and coat pegs.

Bridget huffed. "No, Sis, she saw you do it, and you couldn't pretend you didn't. Like when you —"

"Girlies. Bring your discussion in here. Me aging ears don't hear well from afar, and I shan't be left out."

Cara rose. "I must return Scampers to his bed. Tell her I had to fetch something." She put Scampers away and searched for an item to take to the kitchen. All that came to mind were her recently patched stockings.

"Here she is. Our youngest Muldoon — uh, at home." Aunt Orla blinked and cringed. "Me apologies for that. I know there're other littles we've yet to find."

Bridget and Cara shared a quick glance. "Auntie O, Cara and I wonder about them, and do you have any news? You're bound to hear more than either of us will. We avoid asking Da for fear of upsetting him."

"He doesn't speak of it." Cara took a chair and sat in front of the mound of branches. She wrapped her chilly hands around her hot cup Bridget handed to her.

Orla clucked her tongue. "Ah, now, well he wouldn't wish to, would he? And who can blame him?" She dipped her biscuit, sipped her coffee, then leaned back. Her pale blue eyes sparkled. "Be assured that we adults are doing our best to find them, aye? The latest news is that Moira, Sister Elizabeth, is with a friend examining church records, and Liam is inquiring at nearby schools in his time off. It's tedious work nevertheless, but well worth it, aye? Let me tell you this — your Da monitors the railway chatter, and although he never says, he perseveres. Promise me you'll not nag at him. Do you think you can?"

Cara let out a long sigh. "Hearing this news perks me up like a kitten with a piece of yarn. I hope I can refrain from asking him, although I may not have the patience to wait for news while everyone searches."

Bridget scrunched her eyes closed. "I'm going to pray very hard that one of you finds out where they are. It'll be my Christmas wish as well. I feel so much less sad now. We must be patient, Cara-mite. Don't blow too soon — that reminds me of the time when the dyna-mite for the tunnel —"

"'Tis why you call your sister Cara-mite. 'Twas one of me ques-tions for you." Orla tugged out a piece of greenery and twisted it in the air. "Well, now, we've a pile of shrubbery and branches before us on the table to create something. We'll be needing it cleared by suppertime. Which one of you shall tell me 'bout the clever plan for these?"

With Auntie O's expertise from her childhood's economical Christmas crafts, she taught her nieces all the tricks of using twine and the art of arrangement with nature's plenty. She helped them design to please the eye inside a home. "There now. What do you think?"

Cara grinned. "If we tried this alone, they would've resembled blackberry brambles. Thank you, Auntie O." She lifted a large wreath from the stack. They had a few swags to tie above the doors as well.

"They're beautiful. Only, don't you wish some branches had berries on them? Some red, like for Christmas, would add color and be more striking. I'm sure we have none near us, or do we, Cara?"

Cara shook her head. "Not anywhere nearby. We must work fast, for it's almost noon and we need lunch. My tummy is growling."

"You're always hungry, but we can't stop now. It's too exciting, and you wanted to —"

"Bridget, me girl, you've got a grand idea to add color." Auntie O scooted her chair and stood. "Do you have ribbon in the house? We can use it for decoration. Show me where 'tis."

They plundered every room, even the kitchen, with only Mick's sacrosanct room remaining. All they confiscated were one yellow ribbon, two old bootlaces, and a piece of wire which no one could guess from what.

Cara's tummy growled loud enough to wake the dead, as Auntie O declared, so they made cold plates of cheese, bread, and canned blackberry jam. Cara inspected their Christmas creations stacked before them. "We've wasted an hour trying to find things already, Bridget. Can't we be happy with only greenery? It's more than we began with this morning, and it feels more festive. What else can we use? Our stockings?"

"Aye, Cara. Stockings, or anything we can alter into ornaments." Auntie Orla bit into her bread laden with jam and a chunk of cheese.

Bridget poured them each a glass of water, then sat. "Maybe we could go to the mercantile and find things to use. Right, Auntie O?"

Aunt Orla lifted one brow. "I see you're persisting in getting me back into that mercantile yet, aye? Your town has mayhap grown, nevertheless, I don't expect their manners to be improved."

The discussion was at a standstill until Bridget nearly begged like a dog might for a morsel of meat. "Please think about it, Auntie O? You can undo the rudeness from Mrs. Thompson you received the last time she thought you were turning Moira into, uh, someone like yourself. You're a proper lady now, aren't you? Da says —"

"Oh, give it up, Mount Bridget. Your mention of Da gives me an idea. We've not searched in Da's room for supplies. We should try that." Cara pushed away the guilt knocking on her soul of entering his room without his permission. It's for the worthy cause of encouraging everyone's spirits at Christmastime. She did not want to wait until tomorrow. What was wrong with wanting it all finished while their Aunt Orla visited and could inspire them with the decorations?

Auntie Orla set her cup on the table. "I'm interrupting with the wisdom of elders. 'Tis never acceptable to disobey your father whilst living in his household."

"Didn't expect you to say that." Cara frowned.

"Nevertheless, you'll be making your own choices in this, aye? What do you expect to find?" Aunt Orla grinned — deepening her dimples.

Cara returned her grin. Angel kisses those dimples weren't. I guess she hasn't changed all that much since that first visit.

Bridget scowled. "What are you saying, Auntie O? I don't get it. Yes, to go to the store, or yes to Da's room?"

"Well, now. You're nearly eighteen, and the lady of the house, aye? I'll let you decide."

Cara cradled her head. "That's ruined our project. We'll be here waiting until suppertime."

"Cara-mite, that's not true. I'll choose Da's room first, and if there's nothing for us to use, we can go straight to the store. Right, Auntie O?" Bridget pleaded with a prayer posture.

Aunt Orla upraised her hands. "You've surprised me with the wisdom of King Solomon. Time's a wasting as Cara so aptly complains."

Cara jerked upright. "That's because it's true."

Bridget stood and peered at the hallway. She paced a few times with eager Blackie following while she decided which direction to take. Poor Blackie. All his hopes were pinned onto Bridget as Cara's were. It was the quietest Cara had seen her in a long time.

"Oh, come on, Sis." Cara's nerves could not withstand additional delay, so she stood and busied herself by collecting the dishes and leftovers. "Look at what you've done to her, Auntie O. It's almost cruel."

"Unfair." Orla's eyes widened. "I'd no clue I'd caused so much angst within her."

Bridget paused her pacing. "Clue. That's the thing to help me decide, Auntie O. While we search for Christmas decoration ideas in Da's room, we'll gather clues as to Beth and the boys' whereabouts. She couldn't have taken everything with her."

The women crept after Bridget in single file down the hallway, glancing at Cara in the shadows. She huffed a sigh. "For heaven's sake, Da won't be home for several hours. Why're we being quiet as if he's asleep in his bedroom?"

Bridget tried the doorknob, it turned, and the door swung inward. Sunlight poured through the windows for the room faced west. The other women peeked around her.

One black iron bed, one tall bureau, and one wooden washstand against the far wall. A brass shaving mirror hung beside the window, and Callum's baby crib was where they'd last seen it.

Cara clenched her jaw against the sudden sadness overwhelming her. "This might be a terrible idea. Look at this, Bridget." She approached the crib and fingered one of Callum's blankets. The quilt Beth made for him wasn't there. Nor his teddy.

"His favorite quilt and bear are gone. Hey, Cara. Do you know what this means? No wicked person took them! Beth had time to take his things with her. Let's check for Finn's teddy and blanket."

"Ah, me girlies. So you found some clues. Praise be to God. I'll have a look in the closet, there." Orla opened it and rummaged through the shelves and a few crates while the sisters clung to each other then, dug through the bureau's drawers.

Cara stood up with a pair of little blue mittens Finn had worn. "I don't understand why Da didn't say anything to us about what he stored in here."

"And why would he? Here's something in this one, aye." Aunt Orla lifted a crate and plopped it onto the bed. She blew the dust off the top. "There'd be no reason to stir up the tragedy for you all by telling you what he's kept. They're his remembrances." She opened the crate and peered inside.

The sisters hurried over to Aunt Orla's discovery.

Tucked and stacked inside beneath Beth's yellow gown were tiny stockings, bonnets, and baby gowns for Callum. Short pants and shirts for Finn, and a few caps. More blankets, diapers, and a few toys peeked out from underneath the clothing. Wooden blocks, a red ball, and a yellow rattle.

Cara gulped back a cry and covered her mouth with both hands. The blue mittens dropped to the floor.

Bridget flopped onto the bed beside the crate and sobbed.

Aunt Orla removed the tiny stockings. "I know 'tis part of the heartbreaking tragedy, nevertheless, these are hopeful clues as well, aye? Methinks your little brothers are grand somewhere, and safe. We must hold onto faith and hope in God. Hope pays off, aye?"

Cara sat beside her sister and stroked Bridget's arm. "I suppose you mean not everything is here, and Beth took important items for the boys they'd need. These were not, so she left them." She collected the blue mittens from the floor. "These are tokens for us to remember them."

Aunt Orla tugged out the hidden items to lay beside the now upright Bridget, and Bridget gasped. "Auntie O, Finn loved to throw and chase this ball all around the house day after day."

Cara stroked the smooth, carved wooden horse. "Callum loved to chew on his horse and rattle."

"There 'tis. The best of what we're after. Your dear memories of them come to glorious life. And what better time than at Christmas, don't you know? Pack up the crate and go to the kitchen with those. We shall decorate to our heart's content with your little brothers' toys. I'll show you how, aye?"

***

CHAPTER 5

HER PERFECT CHRISTMAS CHALLENGES

*A*unt Orla asked her nieces to choose where they wanted the wreaths and swags hung, while Bridget set Beth's crate of treasures on the kitchen floor out of their way. "We shall entwine the rattle, ball, and the horse in the branches with their mittens later, aye?"

Cara surveyed the kitchen and common room. "The front door should have a wreath, of course. It's welcoming. But indoors because of the blizzards. One big wind and it could launch it into town where no one would know where it came from."

Bridget pointed to the entry between the common room and kitchen. "A swag could go here. But don't hang it too low, or it'll smack us tall people in the neck. Wouldn't that be terrible? Injured by our own decorations. I heard once at school that someone cut one of those Christmas trees to take home and decorate, but it had an owl living in it. When it flew out at the man it startled him so badly, he had a heart attack and —"

"Mount Bridget, how do you remember these bizarre stories?" Cara scrunched her face.

"Now, Cara, your sister here ought to be a journalist. You mayhap could write articles 'bout all the shocking things people tell you, don't you know? And earn a living at it." Aunt Orla turned to Cara. "Where does your Da keep his nails and hammer?"

"In the barn with his other tools. I'll fetch them." Cara shoved her arms into her coat sleeves and there was another rip. "Fiddle-dee-dee. Bridget, your stitches aren't holding." She twisted around to inspect the arms attached to the back of her coat. Stuffing popped out of a hole around her right shoulder's sleeve. She glanced at the front window. Heavy snowflakes swirled from the sky. "I needed this coat for the senseless winter. Why did God even make Winter?"

Bridget pulled at Cara's torn sleeve. "He's a mystery. You can't go out in that. You'll freeze. Wear my coat. Sorry my mending didn't hold. I don't have the correct thread for your coat. Mary O'Connell says that her ma knows all about threads and you must have the weight that matches your —"

"Yes, yes. Yakity-yak." Cara yanked her arm away from her sister's grip. "I'm sure Mary's right but all I want is to get to the barn so we can finish with our project. Why do you always run the conversation on forever and a day?"

Aunt Orla clapped her hands. "Girlies. There's no grand thing 'about arguing now, aye? It'll slow us down even more. Put on Bridget's coat and get us the supplies, Cara. It'll be grand."

Bridget's coat hung nearly to her ankles. The arms covered her hands by five inches. If she needed a reminder that she was short, this coat did that perfectly. She raised her eyes to the tall chuckling women who were supposed to be her loving family. They tried covering their laughter. It didn't work. "I suppose this is a burden us short people must bear. Nothing we borrow fits us."

"Not to mention you can't reach anything without a ladder. You always ask me to get things for you." Bridget giggled. "And your legs dangle when you're seated in most chairs. The only time you're tall is when you're mounted on horses — hey, that's why you ride! Auntie O, aren't you glad you're tall? I am. I —"

Aunt Orla elbowed Bridget. "We've tormented your short sister enough. Give her two scarves and be sure to wrap them over the hole.

You ought to make haste, Cara, for the snow shan't wait for you. Nonetheless, we can wait until tomorrow, aye?"

"No. I'll go now." Cara shook her bundled up arms. "Blackie, stay. I can do this by myself. Although I'm short. Short people are mighty dynamite without being able to reach anything or see over people in a gathering, right, Mount Bridget?"

Aunt Orla shooed Cara out the door. "Me only sister was a shortie, and I loved her to pieces. You'll do grand. Nevertheless, should you sink into the snow we shan't find you until Spring, aye? Don't be doing none of that, if you please."

Cara slammed the door and stomped down the steps that had accumulated a few inches of snow. *I'd best hurry.* Something moved within her side vision. She stopped and squinted through the falling snow. What was it? *Did I imagine it? Wish I'd brought Da's rifle. Should I turn back?*

Unease returned to Cara's mind, but the livestock was quiet. Everything was hushed except for the plop of snowflakes hitting the earth. She was almost to the barn. Again, something moved past. Snarling accompanied it this time, and she screeched as she jerked on the doors in panic. An object collided against a door. "Dear God, in heaven, keep me safe!" She slammed the doors and barred them with her shaky hands. Her entire body trembled, and she inhaled quick gulps of air.

Wings paced and tossed his head up with a whinny.

Once she calmed down, she noted the restlessness of the other animals. Buttercup lowed and shifted her weight on her hooves. Plus the sheep and chickens skittered around their respective pens. Their tension beckoned to her for reassurance. "Don't worry, everybody, I'll keep you safe from harm. And myself." She'd feed them early and come up with a plan to get back to the house before dark.

After she gave her creatures the care they required, she checked her skirt pocket for Scampers. Gone. *He must've fell out when I was scared out of my wits! This is terrible.* She sagged onto a hale bale. Tears trickled down her cheeks. *Poor defenseless thing. What would happen to him?* She sobbed for the tiny mouse and for her little brothers. They were like the cute little mouse that needed big people's protection.

Baaing from the sheep pen grabbed Cara's attention. She wiped her face and nose. "What's upsetting you now, fluffy woolies? You're more nervous than me, and I had a frightful encounter with a predator."

The closer she drew to the sheep's pen, it became apparent some paws dug in the snow at the base of the barn's wall, accompanied by loud sniffing.

Cara rushed to the pitchfork and shovel. She grasped them in each hand and hurried to the wall. She banged the shovel flat against the boards and yelled as loud as possible. It was one time it was acceptable to frighten your own sheep and the rest of the barnyard.

The expected chaos from her animals ensued. Then Blackie furiously barked outside. Did he escape from the house? She screamed. "No, Blackie!"

The barn doors burst open with Aunt Orla and Bridget holding onto them with panicked expressions. "What's happening? We heard you scream, and saw something run toward the barn doors. We thought you were being killed, we did." Aunt Orla dropped her big branch that came from the creek. Bridget kept hers in hand.

"Where's Blackie? There're wolves or coyotes or something out there. Blackie!"

The beloved sheepdog rushed into the barn to Cara. She sobbed all over him and Bridget did as well.

"Cara, there's no blood. I think he's uninjured." Bridget ruffled his fur.

"Good dog. He didn't want to leave us alone for long, only to protect us." Cara sniffed.

Aunt Orla snatched the pitchfork and disappeared outside. She returned a moment later. "Aye, there're several kinds of tracks all-round the barn there. We'd best lock up and get back to your home, don't you know. 'Tis turning dark."

Cara collected the shovel and handed the hammer and nails to Bridget. "We'll each have a weapon for the trek home. Be watchful, but I think it's scared off." After securing the doors, and shoving the rock against them, she led the way home. Large snowflakes stuck to her eyelashes. Their boot prints had filled in fast with the fresh fallen snow. "Let's pray Da stays in town for the night. There's no way to warn him of the danger."

Once inside the safety and warmth of their home, Cara had difficulty focusing on her special project of Christmas decorating. All the excitement drained out of it by the danger she had dealt with and the loss of Scampers. She draped herself over Blackie on the chilly floor rug. The draft through the doorjamb urged her to take the dog to the kitchen by the warm stove and where Aunt Orla relaxed at the table with some coffee.

"Let's all thaw out, aye? I set the pot to boiling for us."

"I lost Scampers outside." Cara sniffled.

"Who would that be, now?" Aunt Orla paused her cup in front of her face and blew on the steam.

"A pet I kept in the house."

Bridget collected more wood and kindling from the wood box attached to the kitchen. "That' so sad. He might return when it warms up in here." She stacked some kindling within the coals inside the kitchen's cook stove. "I'm sorry I allowed the fires in the stoves to burn so low during today's excitement. It'll be warm in no time. At least it's not as bad as Mrs. Longan said it could get. She let her fires burn out once for so long that all her doors froze shut, and her windows grew ice on them so thick, it didn't melt until Spring thaw, and it took her hours to —"

"Bridget. Here's your coffee, aye? You're our most dedicated Muldoon for keeping the home fires burning." Aunt Orla pushed a chair out with her foot. "Sit when you're done and we'll discuss what comes after."

When the three Muldoon women settled at the table, Cara leaned in. "I wonder what to do about, Da. Do you have any ideas? Will he know to stay in town in this weather? We've lived through many Dakota plains winters, but I'm anxious for him."

"He knows I'm here and shall know to be safe himself." Aunt Orla stirred her coffee and milk.

Bridget grimaced. "People often think they know better and go out in blizzards to take care of something and still go missing. I can tell you I'd not do such a thing. Da knows we can take care of ourselves, so I think he'd not risk his own safety, right?" She stared out the kitchen window at the white flakes which blew past. "Remember Mr. Howard and how they found him in the —"

"Girlie." Aunt Orla squinted. "'Tis best not to be speaking of these morbid events just now, aye? Our Cara here looks unwell. Methinks we should get back to the decorating, then put out our supper. That'll cheer us all up grand, aye?"

Cara sighed and rubbed her face. "You're right, Auntie O. I've been afraid and sidetracked and it's tired me out. It's too early to go to bed. I don't know about cheering up but it might take our minds off Da out there in the snow. But I don't think so."

Bridget scrunched her eyes closed. "Let's pray together like Moira taught us to do whenever we were afraid."

They prayed and said amen together, and Cara admitted she felt a smidgeon better. If God can't do something about Da then no one could. She selected the wreath for the door and turned it over. "I wish we'd red ribbon to weave through it. Does it look Christmasy enough do you think?"

"Of course it does, me doubting niece. Do you know why we Irish hang wreaths made from the beauty that grows in nature? Because all nature celebrates God creating it." Aunt Orla lifted the hammer and nails from the table and carried them to Cara. "Show me where you wish it hung."

Bridget finished inserting more wood into the common room stove's belly and joined them. "Here." She poked her finger well above Cara's head.

"Not there. Here." Cara shoved Bridget's finger down about nine inches.

"What? Only elves could see it then, Cara. Da keeps saying we've got Fairies or Brownies in the house, but we're not decorating for them. They don't care about such things. But I'm beginning to believe him. Did you know that when I went into the kitchen the other day —"

"Mount Bridget. I'm not as short as elves or Brownies, but as the shortest in the family, I can't enjoy the wreath way above my head."

Orla pounded a nail into the wood. "As your guest, I'm putting an end to your shameful squabble and choosing where it hangs, aye? Halfway between tall and short shall do the trick."

Bridget snorted, snatched the other wreath, and rushed into the kitchen. "This one goes on the center of the table. All we need is a candle. Now, where did we put the other matches?" She disappeared down the hallway to the rooms.

"We eat and do use the table all the time. I think she should find a better spot. Auntie O, let's hang the swags." Cara gathered them and scanned the common room. "One over the window and one over the cabinet?"

A high-pitched howl echoed around the house. Cara dropped the swags and clutched her aunt's arms. They clung to each other, as Bridget rushed to them with a lit lantern.

Blackie's ruff stood on end. He growled and sniffed and pawed at the door.

"Dear God, keep our da away from the house tonight." Bridget embraced her quaking sister and aunt. "How can we drive them away?"

Cara broke Bridget's embrace and hurried to Mick's bedroom. She grabbed his rifle from the wall and checked for ammunition. It was loaded and her hands trembled. She'd only shot it for target practice a few times. But she knew how. She gripped Mick's gun, barrel faced down and headed for the entry.

Bridget gasped as Cara ran past her. "Are you sure you should even open the —"

"Cara." Auntie Orla grasped her free arm. "Remember to aim above the barn and avoid the porch roof as well."

Cara twisted the knob, readied the rifle, and carefully slid the barrel through the tight gap. She angled the weapon ten degrees upward and fired. The recoil thrust her back, bruising her shoulder. Her ears rang like Christmas church bells.

"How do we know we're safe, sister?" Bridget cringed on the floor and clung to Blackie. "I've never heard anything so noisy in all my life. Was it enough to keep them away? I heard that hungry wolves hunt in packs and they're braver than coyotes. Kendra Halloran says —"

"Mount Bridget, we're always safe inside our home, but the snow has let up and Da might be on his way. They're intelligent animals, and they'll remember the gunshot for a long time. Right, Auntie O?" Cara leaned the gun against the wall and rubbed her ears.

Aunt Orla massaged her own ears, then shrugged. "I know little 'bout wolves' behavior, only a bit from living in Minnesota. We'd none in Ireland, thank the Almighty. 'Tis an island in the Atlantic."

"Luck of the Irish."

"That saying leaves a lot to be desired in me own estimation. Never quite understood it, aye?"

"Well, I think it means several things." Bridget raised her hand and ticked a fingertip. "One, they can make their own luck. Two, people wonder how the Irish got their luck. Three, they've survived so many dreadful tragedies it defies imagination. Four —"

"Aye. You've spoken enough valid points there."

Cara grasped the rifle and lantern again, then headed for the outdoors. "I must see to our livestock, and check if they've settled after the gunshot."

"Ho there. Not alone. I've got me pitchfork, and Bridget's got the shovel. Lead the way."

With the snowstorm passed, its wake left millions of uncovered bright stars. Cara's mood lightened with the clear sky's beauty caressing the prairie's hills. "Stars of wonder. That song makes so much sense now." She hummed the Christmas carol, and her family joined in with the words — their frosty breaths swirled upward. Her chilled lips restrained her own participation.

When they entered the barn, the creatures' agitation stirred her heart. *They depend upon my presence and care to soothe them.* "Me, a fifteen-year-old." To them, a child is the one with the power. Astonishing.

"The power to do what?" Bridget caressed Buttercup's back while the cow chewed her cud. "You know, I hadn't thought much about it before, but we've got our own Christmas manger scene. We have the cow, sheep, horses and chickens. Oh, and the kittens. All it needs now is Baby Jesus. Isn't that funny? Every rancher and farmer have the makings of their own modern manger in their own barns."

"You forgot the angels, me lovely niece. What's a Christmas scene without those glorious creatures, aye?" Aunt Orla stroked Wings' cheeks as he snuffled her shoulder and scarf. "We need them now, aye?"

Sweet women of mine. "I'm glad you left out the wolves. This is one of your best ramblings I've heard in a long time." Cara wrapped her arms around Bridget's waist. "I think I'll listen to your rambling more closely in the future."

Bridget embraced her little sister. "Promise?"

"Not exactly." Cara grimaced. "Maybe I can keep my promise until the day after Christmas?"

***

CHAPTER 6

HER FEARS FORTIFIED

*C*ara awoke to voices and footsteps which echoed down the hallway from the common room. Her women folk had stayed up close to midnight creating ornaments from nature and Beth's discarded belongings of their little brothers. Her eyes stung with the effort, yet the results were cheerful for her heart. *What time is it?* Her bedroom window let no daylight in. She yawned and scooted out from under her warm covers and into the chilly air. One more week until Christmas Eve.

A low-timbered voice mixed with Bridget's. "Da!" Cara hurried to put on her slippers and tugged her quilt off the bed to wrap herself in it. She ran, then slid down the hallway, her flailing grip missed the corner, and she landed on her rump at the end of it. Her quilt flew over her head and covered her face. Someone unwrapped her. "Hi, Da."

His weathered, whiskered face, adorned by a long half gingered half white mustache, swept across his jutting chin, and accentuated his broad grin. "*Macushla*. Me own dear Cara. Always one to give us silly antics, aye?" He tugged her to her feet. "Was on me way to get you up, sleepyhead."

Cara grabbed hold of her father and squeezed him until tears trickled down her cheeks and her arms ached. "I was so afraid for you last night and hoped you'd stay in town."

"And so I did. Stabled Thunderstorm — Storm, with Billy and slept at the Horan's home." Mick draped his arm across his youngest's shoulders. "You were you the one to shoot last night? We heard it at the Holoran's. What's this tale of wolves and guns and staying up until all hours? 'Tis years since you rebuffed your bedtime, aye?"

"It was your gun I shot. They ran off." Cara wrinkled her nose at him. "And Da, I get tired now. Back then there were so many people at home to play with." A sudden longing for those days gripped her heart and choked her.

Aunt Orla and Bridget poked their heads through the kitchen entry. "Now isn't this grand? A da and his girlie reunited after one whole day. To be sure, 'twas a frightful night. Nevertheless, here we all are safe and sound by God's own angels."

Cara released her father. "I must see to the livestock."

Mick waved his hand and winked. "Aye, you must. You'll find that I've stabled Storm and fed our horses and left the rest for you out of me kind heart. I must be away to the crew soon." He took a step and turned back to Cara. "When do you return to school? I've lost track. You're the only one left at school age."

"No, Da. We've two more. Finn is almost school age. Callum will follow a year after." Cara tucked in her lips and gulped back a silent sob.

Her father's blue eyes glistened with tears. "Right you are. 'Twas thoughtless to say such a thing. I'm grateful for your recollection and resilience in hoping." He laid his warm palm on her head, then turned back toward the lit kitchen and breakfast.

Cara bundled up with Bridget's huge coat, and her own work boots. *No sense asking my sister, she won't need it, she's inside where it's cozy.* Toasty. Her tummy growled. Buttered toast with blackberry jam. *Stop it.* The perking coffee already assailed her nostrils and was tempting enough.

"Cara-mite, take a hot drink with you." Bridget handed her a steaming cup and sent her a dimpled smile. "You deserve it after last night. Hurry back though, before Auntie O eats all the biscuits. You know how she hoards them."

"Thank you, sis." Cara collected the lit lantern from the table under the window.

Blackie padded over to Cara to beg to accompany her as he did every day. "Why he simply must go out with me is beyond my understanding."

Bridget shrugged. "You'd know better than I would."

"Doggy determination and loyalty are a mystery to us people. I know I can safely say that I wouldn't go out there with you if I could choose. Are you sure you wish to freeze off your wagging tail? Or maybe you've not forgotten last night's scare."

The pair stepped onto the covered porch, and the frozen air assaulted her eyes. Everything was covered with layer upon layer of ice. It must be nearing dawn. The light directly above the furthest horizon increased to light blue fading up into indigo where the shining night stars refused to be budged by the sun. Although who wouldn't enjoy the winter sending a perfect clear day again?

Tracks in the snow marred the picturesque scene. She took a deep breath and wondered if the pack would return. The Muldoon farm was small, but it provided ample delights for starving predators. Their hunger only required one stray sheep. Or a couple of escaped chickens. She must ask her father about reinforcements for the barn walls. "Something must work to protect our critters beyond sleeping in the barn with them."

Once inside the structure, she hurried through her tasks with the livestock and inspected the wall's base nearest the coop and the sheep pen. No gaps or holes. Cara took the lantern and Blackie a second time around the barrier protecting their creatures to check on its condition before she headed home for breakfast.

"Now let's check for problems outside, Blackie, and report any to Da." Her footfalls crunched in the icy snow. She bent down with the lantern to highlight the wood planks where she estimated the coop and pen were on the other side and found teeth and claw marks. Not good at all. "Da will know what to do, right Blackie?"

The alert sheepdog sniffed the air. His nose twitched but his hackles didn't rise. It was time to go.

When Cara and companion returned to the kitchen, Aunt Orla clapped her hands in delight. "At last. Relieved to see you, I am, after our scare last night. We've been telling your da how brave you were. He seems entirely unsurprised."

Mick scraped up the last bite on his plate and took a swig of coffee. "Our Cara has always been made of resilient stuff." He slid a glance at her. "And now Bridget named you Cara-mite. Aptly so, aye?" He slid his chair away from the table and stood. "Me crew expects me soon, and I must be away. Were the animals grand? Are there any needs?"

Cara nodded as she sat in front of her empty plate. "They were fine. But the barn needs repair or reinforcement, Da. I found claw marks and bite marks on the wood near the pens. They've also dug in spots. Do you think it'll hold up against their hunger?"

Bridget gasped. "This is why I am an indoor daughter. If I saw all that and had to come up with a plan, I'd forever have nightmares. I like creatures, but not the predators. Do you know that —"

"Unhelpful, me girlie." Mick stood and handed Bridget his empty plate and cup. "This is life on the prairie. They were here before us, and modernization, and hunting creates vicious lack for them. We know 'bout lack and hunger in Ireland. I'll return for supper, *macushlas*. And Cara, do your best to protect our livestock until we can reinforce the structure. There's a good girlie."

Aunt Orla lifted her last biscuit and grimaced. "The hunger in Ireland? Holy heavens, 'twas a terrible thing. Don't wish to think 'bout it ever again."

Bridget huffed. "But those were the people, Auntie O. Not scary wildlife —"

"Are you sure of that, me darling?" Aunt Orla chuckled. "They're all the same to me, so I've experienced."

"No. They're not the same. I think Cara must get out more around actual people and not only have animals for friends. The perfect Christmas event for her is in a few days. It's a Christmas dance. Don't

47

you think she should go? I am. Let me find the invitation." Bridget clambered around the kitchen tugging open the cabinet drawers. "Where did I put it?"

Cara scooted out her chair and went to the stove to dish up the eggs and pancakes herself. "It's at Josie Halloway's house. I'm not at all intrigued by that. She's a rude, conceited girl without a heart, plus a dance in a stuffy house isn't my idea of fun."

Aunt Orla took her plate and cup to the sink. She looked out the window. "What do you think 'bout me own idea of fun? Whilst it's another clear day, and before I leave you, let's take a trip to the mercantile, aye? We shall finish ornamenting your wreaths and swags, and I wish to add another Christmas gift for each of you to the ones I brought with me. We shall be a merry threesome."

"I know Bridget will be thrilled."

Bridget returned to the kitchen with a cream envelope in her grasp. "It's turning out to be a lovely day, because I found our invitation in my sewing basket — no idea how it got there, but here it is, Cara. Do you know Da gave me some money from his winnings for the household? What shall I get with it? Maybe I'll know when I see it. I love to shop." She grinned in glee.

Cara scrunched her nose. "I don't. But I'll do it for you." She breathed a deep breath. "I can't be away for more than a few hours. Da charged me with keeping watch on our critters. You heard him."

Bridget flicked her hand. "I did. Time to get dressed. What shall we wear? I think our wool stockings I laundered are dry by now. Do you know, Auntie O, it once took five days for them to dry? I can tell you —"

"Only five days? Back in Ireland, it would take a week." Aunt Orla followed Bridget out of the room but turned around to wink at Cara when she joined them.

"It once took ten days for my braided hair to dry. I'll take a risk and braid it again." Cara chuckled.

"Cara-mite, leave it loose for once. I'd give up all the eggs for the next month of breakfasts to have your long, curly hair. Mine is fine and stick straight."

"I'm too practical to leave it loose."

Dressed in their finery an hour later, the women climbed into the sleigh while Cara held onto magnificent Wings. The sleigh only fit four people, so it was perfect with room for Blackie. They covered themselves with wool blankets, and Cara urged Wings forward.

The winter sun hung low over the eastern horizon with enough intensity to reflect off the snow. Cara squinted until her eyes were slits and lowered her leather hat's brim to provide some shade.

Wings, being a sturdy Percheron, always towed the sleigh with ease, and the winter contraption skated smoothly over the icy snow and hills two miles into the railroad town.

Cara closed her eyes for a moment to savor the calming motion.

Bridget said, "Let's sing carols. How about, *One Horse Open Sleigh*? It's perfect, don't you think? 'Jingle bells, jingle bells—'"

After two rounds, Aunt Orla suggested *Christmas Bells* next. "Always been fond of it since 'twas written during the Civil War, a few years before I arrived in America."

They approached the little town on the next hill, and Wings eagerly increased his pace.

Bridget squealed. "My heavens, how fast are we going, and why?"

Cara spoke over her shoulder. "He's been to town enough times to know that Billy's brushing and sweet feed await him at the stables. I don't need to hurry him up."

"Glorious creatures, are the horses, aye?" Aunt Orla shifted forward by grasping Cara's seat. "You do well as a driver. Methinks your heart is very much in it, me girlie. You should always be a horsewoman."

Bridget snorted. "Her heart is into horses, that's true, but it's also into a young man named Billy Horan. Mark my words."

"What's this? You've got a fella and haven't said a word to your own Auntie?"

Cara's heart thumped and her annoyance bristled. "Bridget, you take that back. We've no understanding whatsoever, and Da would choke on his mustache if he heard you say such a thing. I'm too young to have a fella. We're friends and been so since First Grade."

"Sure." Bridget giggled.

Cara flushed from her neck to her cheeks. Silly sister. Why must she tease like this in front of Auntie O? She'll certainly tell Da. "Don't say anything in front of Billy, please?"

As predicted, Wings tugged the full sleigh down Main Street right up to the stables without her directing him.

Cara gathered her blanket and tossed it onto the pile behind her. She stood to climb down, when two black boots entered her side vision. She stared over her shoulder into Billy Horan's sky blue, twinkling eyes, and missed her step.

Billy broke her ungraceful fall with his strong arms and set her down upright. He grinned at her but didn't tease. "Good morning, Miss Muldoon. Your Wings there, is sure determined to get what he wants. Didn't even wait for me to lead him inside."

Cara gulped with a dry throat. "The sweet feed. It's that and your brush. I was telling my family as we drove down the street. You know my sister Bridget, and this is my Auntie Orla come for a visit."

He tipped his hat. "Nice to meet you. I'd better get in. How long will you be?"

Bridget handed Billy some coins from her purse. "Maybe two hours. We'll be at the mercantile shopping. Come on, Auntie O, Cara can catch up with us later."

Billy turned to Cara. "You know what care I give to the horses, but is there anything else I can do for you? Are you going to the Christmas dance? I hope —"

"No. Bye." Cara waved and dashed after her family down the street and across the way. "Wait for me, Bridget!"

A limited number of shoppers, women bundled up for winter weather in reds, greens, or blues, entered the Main Street Mercantile. Although a week before Christmas, there simply weren't many women in town other than the rail worker's wives and daughters. It had always been so in Cara's life.

A fancier equipage than the Muldoon's sleigh pulled up and Josie and her mother stepped down dressed in their city finery with Josie's older brother's help. *Arthur. That was his name.*

Josie spied Cara as she slowed her steps. *This should ruin my day.* Cara paused and nearly returned to the stables.

"Hello, Miss Muldoon. Mother, you know Mr. Mick Muldoon, don't you? This is his youngest daughter." Ugly malice glittered in Josie's green eyes.

Mrs. Holloway lifted her nose and looked Cara up and down. *She no doubt resents Da parting with a bit of her money.*

Bridget peeked out the shop door and waved Cara in. "What are you waiting for? We've already found a few things. It's so exciting. Hurry." She retreated inside and a bell tinkled.

"Mother and I are shopping last minute items for my Christmas dance. We've run out of things because our home is absolutely bursting with cheer. So why have you come to town?"

Cara purposely shivered and avoided Mrs. Holloway's snobby gaze. "The same idea. It's too cold to stand out here." *Colder than an iceberg with the Holloway women present.* "I'm going inside." She hurried to open the door, and the bell announced her entry.

Josie's loud whisper was more like a train whistle. "Mother, she couldn't help being rude to us. Did you see her torn and dirty coat? It's from the missionary barrel, don't you think? Someone should've laundered and mended it first. She must've been freezing out on the street. Poor thing. You always say to be charitable."

Mrs. Holloway muttered and followed Cara inside.

Aunt Orla sidled up to Cara. "This visit to the store brings back memories of another visit when I brought all of you girlies here for the dress and the boots, aye?" She raised her voice. "'Tis as I expected here. Some towns never change for the better for the people in them don't. Shame on them. Let me take you to Bridget."

Bridget carried a basket full of colored ribbons in various widths and sizes. Yellow, red and green. "These shall be perfect to add to our wreaths and swags. What do you think of these sparkling gold stars, Cara? Only a few, but don't they remind you of the star over the manger? I'm looking for angels everywhere. Do you see any? Or candy canes would also work."

Aunt Orla and Cara searched bins and items on the walls in what appeared to be the Christmas decoration section. Cara snatched the last delicate angel ornament. "Here's an angel."

"And here're the candy canes at last, me girlies. Seemed odd for the shop to have none at Christmastime." Aunt Orla stood before a row of assorted candy bins and collected the three canes at the bottom of one. She blew off a small dust ball. "Are these from last year, then?"

Bridget handed the basket of ribbons to Cara. "Hold these. I just remembered we need more flour if we're to make Christmas cookies. Wait here."

Josie approached Aunt Orla and extended her palm between them. "My sincerest apologies, ma'am, but the shopkeeper forgot to add these to our bag. My mother previously paid for all of them for my Christmas dance treats. You understand, don't you? I know Cara does."

Cara nodded yet clenched her fists inside her gloves gripping the basket handle even tighter. "I do."

"I understand what's happening as well, aye. In these difficult situations, we shall always do well to remember that God in heaven sees everything, don't you know, young lady?" Aunt Orla's pale eyes flashed a fire within them that could light the kindling in the cook stove.

"Josie, come to me at once." Mrs. Holloway's voice pierced like a whistle. It would be terrible to live with that.

After Josie departed with her mother, Cara stamped her boot. "I want to scream like a girl."

Aunt Orla said, "You are one, girlie. And it won't help to have fits. I've met many a woman like those two, and you shall as well. Never forget to be the better person, and you'll do grand. You'll see."

Bridget hauled a bag of flour past and headed for the cash register counter. "Of whom are you speaking of? See what? Well, I'm ready to go. This trip was much quicker than I expected, and we can finish our projects before Auntie O leaves. Aren't you happy we've encountered no problems finding what we wanted and how —"

"Mount Bridget, my dear sister, I'd love to be as clueless as you. The world is desperate for your innocent outlook."

"I guess that sounds nice. I know you must be desperate for a new coat. But I forgot to mention that I asked about ones to fit you, Cara-mite, and they're plumb out of any smaller sizes. I'm sorry, Sis, but we can pray for a warm, pretty coat as a Christmas gift."

Cara scuffed her boots along the floor until they traipsed outside to the stables. "With my luck it would be a hideous red."

***

CHAPTER 7

HER CHRISTMAS MOOD

The day after Aunt Orla departed, and six days before Christmas Eve, Cara fought with her swirling emotions surrounding the most important holiday. She didn't want to miss her family, like the boys, Moira and Liam, or to worry about Scampers and his fate, but no amount of telling herself not to feel that way worked. "I just plain miss them and want everyone home for Christmas."

Cara sifted through her bureau drawers for the umpteenth time. Nothing. Scampers hadn't reappeared where she could find him for days, and Bridget couldn't care less. Her sister and father did not want him inside at all. Auntie O seemed to understand her bents, but she was gone and lived hundreds of miles away in Minnesota.

What time is it? She leaned close to her bedroom window and swiped the fog off to peer outside. Midday? People at work. Dreary white clouds, and white hills speckled with random shrubs or a tree. One lone small gray cloud out toward town. Near the school, maybe? She turned away to face her bedroom. She could go for a ride into town. Or help Bridget with the laundry. That's desperate. Cara plopped onto her bed at the same time her bedroom door squeaked open. "Blackie. Come here, sweet boy, and thanks for looking for me.

I didn't want to be alone." He always had a special way of knowing when she needed him.

The dog whined yet refused to climb up on the bed. "I bet you want me to get you out. I give in." Cara swung her legs off the bed and followed him as he led the way. They passed Bridget's door, and Cara peeked inside. "I'm taking Blackie out and going for a quick ride. Are you reading on laundry day?"

Bridget didn't glance in her direction and kept her attention on the book. "Uh, huh. I'm to the part where," she turned a page, "they found the skeleton. That took long enough. Doing laundry in a minute."

"That girl enjoys a creepy mystery. Me? Not so much. Real life is mysterious enough. I'll help you with washing after my ride."

Blackie eyed Cara for any clues whether she was staying to chat longer but kept going.

Once they arrived at the barn, Cara used the daylight to check the reinforcement project she had helped Mick and his friends, Flash and Wolf, finish the previous evening. "Looks secure, Blackie. It took very little time with the four of us. Our critters should be safe for the rest of the winter." *Eases my fears for them.*

Alone, Wings whinnied to her from inside — her father had ridden Storm to work as usual. Wings' greeting set the chickens and sheep to creating added cacophony. "They won't convince me to feed them again, no matter how loud they squawk at me. No begging, right Blackie?"

He stared at her and woofed.

Cara readied Wings for their jaunt and sat on the edge of his stall to mount him. "It'll be a quick trip while the weather holds, but we'll be free to fly and clear our heads on the plains. Blackie, are you ready?"

He circled the barn floor, keeping his intelligent stare on her and the horse. He knew what came next, and his eagerness tightened his muscles. Even Tricky and Boo scrambled away from the door, for they also sensed what Cara planned. Hadn't they witnessed it many times before?

"Ready, set, go!" She urged Wings forward through the open

double doors, and the dog stayed on their heels. They surged out and down the gentle slope on the shoveled path her father always cleared for travel into town. She'd pull up Wings where the path ended. Being born and raised in these prairie hills, she knew every dell and which snow-covered pitfalls to avoid. Wings did too, but riders have responsibilities to their mounts.

The thundering horse beneath her saddle and the pounding of his rhythmic hooves soothed and blew away the darkest places from her soul. Her long braid thumped a slower beat against her back. Wind slammed her covered face, freeing her of her worries for the moment, and she was one with the earth, sky, and all God's creation. Cara's body was only one part of her. The rest of her was ethereal, and her speed over the hills meant no worries could reach her.

At the end of the shoveled pathway, she slowed Wings' pace. They came upon it too fast for her desire. "Thank you, Wings. That was glorious."

Blackie panted and his tongue lolled out one side of his muzzle, yet his eyes sparkled with enjoyment, she was sure.

The invigorated threesome trod through about a foot of snow headed to Main Street. What is that odd tendril of gray spinning into the sky? It isn't a cloud after all, is it? It could only be — "A fire!"

Cara rushed Wings to the quiet and deserted Main Street, then quickly up to Horan's Stable, with Blackie barking to awaken the sleepy town.

"Billy, come quick!"

Billy hurried out to meet them at the hitching post outside the stable doors.

"Do you see a fire? There. Or is it my imagination?" She waited for his answer, while Wings shuffled and foamed at his bit.

Billy raised his hat brim and studied what Cara had believed was a tendril of gray cloud but up close, was a glowing cloud now billowing up with sparks drifting near the base. "Holy cow, it is a fire. You stay here. I'm telling my father."

The acrid scent of smoke blew in their direction on the breeze.

What could they do? Everyone was at work except for a few men with businesses in town. Not enough men to fight a fire, surely.

"I'm not waiting. Go, Wings. Fly!" Cara leaned over his withers and held on tight. The saddlebow pushed against her stomach. She ignored it. She had no plan other than to get closer to discover what was burning. It was at the end of the road, so it was the school or the church. "Let there be no one inside, God."

Visible orange flames now shone at the rear of the school, and the closer Cara and Wings drew to the fire, the horse slowed and resisted her urging him forward. He skidded to a standstill and refused to budge further.

A portion of the schoolhouse's roof caved in with a crash. Cara listened for anyone calling out for help, but the fire's crackling hunger drowned out any other sounds. She must find some men and fast. After turning Wings back downtown, she spied Billy and three men running toward her and the school. Mr. Horan, Mr. Sully from the Supply Store and the shopkeeper, Mr. Thompson. They brandished snow shovels. Hope they're enough.

Cara slid quickly to the ground and towed Wings to a nearby tree to hitch him in front of the church while she did whatever she could to help the men. Flakes fell around her as she ran, and she turned her face upward, expecting snow. They stung. "Ow! What?"

Mr. Horan yelled, "Stay back. These tiny embers can ignite clothing and hair. Stay clear of them, aye? Can you get around to the side of the church? We must know whether the fire has spread. Quickly, now." He sped to the other men hastily shoveling snow and tossing it onto the flames at the rear of the school.

Her heart thudded hard and fast. She gulped in heated breaths. The smoke choked her, so she wound her scarf tightly over her face. Please, God, keep everyone safe from the fire.

Around the back of the building, she frantically ran to check for flames with Blackie on her flank. The church bell suddenly pealed, and it resounded with an alarm unimaginable. Soon, the entire community would take notice of the disaster happening among them.

Father Calhoun rushed out the church's back door, and nearly into Cara. He grasped her arms. "Are you injured?"

She shook her head, coughed, and her throat burned. "Not much. Are you?"

"Nay, Miss Muldoon. How did you come to be here at a time like this?" His anxious expression and quick glances at the school unnerved her. He tugged her backward a few steps when another portion of a wall caved in. "You shouldn't be here, aye? What shall your da say 'bout your being in danger?"

"I saw the fire and told Billy." She coughed again. "I wanted to help somehow." Her lungs burned, and she coughed. "I don't have a shovel —"

"Ah now, you've surely helped already, make no mistake." He squeezed her arms. "Without your quick as a wink warning, 'twould be much worse, aye? Away from the smoke with you. I'll be helping them." He took wide steps in the snow toward his fellow men.

Where to go? To the men, although Father Calhoun said to stay away, or to Wings, who surely needed attention. She ought not to worry about Blackie. He'd never leave her side. "Loyal to the extreme, aren't you, boy?" She coughed.

When Cara and the dog returned to Wings, the Percheron snuffled in distress. "I'm sorry to leave you, and I know fire is as terrifying for you as it is for people. Maybe worse." She stroked his white velvety nose, then hugged his neck. "You were a magnificent help in getting us here. I'll always remember your courage today."

From the several men working frantically and joined by a few others who had heard the church bell, it appeared they won their furious battle to keep the fire from spreading to the church. They all stayed alert for any stray embers and sparks drifting with the fire's own unpredictable wind. Cara guarded the church.

She scooped a glove full of snow and held it against the stinging spots on her face. "How silly I am to think they were snowflakes? Maybe the burns will blend in with my freckles." Her devoted friends, Wings and Blackie, paid no attention to her murmurs while she led Wings back and forth on Main Street to belatedly cool him down.

Mrs. Thompson from the mercantile passed her with two ladies bearing water and cookies for the men resting on the church steps. They ignored Cara.

Oh, no, Bridget. "She must be worried about me. Don't know how long I've been gone."

Billy dragged his shovel behind him and leaned it against the stable wall. He approached Cara when she drew Wings to the hitching post near the stables. His close inspection of her made her squirm a little. "Lucky thing your coat didn't catch on fire." He indicated her arm. "Could've been worse. And your hat. It's singed as well. I'd say your guardian angel did his job."

Cara scanned her sleeves and removed her hat. Small burn holes dotted her already torn sleeves, and her leather hat had soot smeared on it. "I guess he must've. You're singed on the edges as well. Black suits your pale skin and especially that sudden mustache and beard you're wearing."

His clear complexion, except for the spots with soot smeared all over it, blushed a deep crimson.

Why did I tease him? Her own face heated. She spun her hat over and brushed her fingers over the ashes. That made it worse.

Billy cleared his throat and coughed. "You were brave, Cara. The men were talking about you and said the school would be gone without your warning." He tugged off his hat, which made his black hair stand up like crow's feathers, plus he gave her a bow. He offered her his bent elbow. "Come with me."

Being fawned over by a group of grown men unsettled her. She listened to their praise and honor until it was too much. "I don't get it. No need to praise me. Half the school is gone."

Mr. Horan patted her arm. "Aye, but 'tis better than the entirety, aye, men? We'll be telling the tale for years to come of how a young lady warned this town of the impending disaster and saved it from sure destruction."

No wonder Mr. Horan and Da are friends. They sound the same. Irishmen — a different breed of men. If they were an animal, they'd be a mixture of unicorns, cuddly puppies, and grizzly bears.

***

On the prairie, one can see for miles, so of course Da was home already. Cara goaded Wings faster when they encountered the cleared path to their home.

Three unfamiliar horses besides Storm, tied to the porch rails, turned their heads to greet Wings. Some of Da's rail crew must be here. Great. More questions. Cara sighed and coughed. She was too tired to talk about the fire again.

Bridget and Mick rushed onto the porch. Mick reached Cara first and nearly smothered her in his fierce embrace. "Macushla. Our Cara. I was just told the tale in town." He moved her to arm's length and stared at her up and down with tears brimming. "Are you well? They said you were well. We rode toward the smoke and discovered it was our town. They said you left. We hurried like deer away from wolves to get here, and you weren't —"

"Da. I'm fine. I really wasn't anywhere near to the fire itself."

"Nonetheless, you look singed. Doesn't she, Bridget?" He removed Cara's hat.

Bridget grabbed her shoulders for a hug. "I was so relieved to see Da come home until I heard his story. You said, a ride. Not a fire. For heaven's sake. Why do these things happen to you? I couldn't believe it when —"

Cara burst into sobs. *Why? I'm fine.* She shook uncontrollably.

"Our hero Cara must have a moment to herself, aye? She's grand. No worries there." Da gripped her arm and tugged her, with Blackie following, into their home and away from the onlookers lined up on the porch. "Bridget, can you fetch our Cara-mite a tea? Preferably a calming one?" He drew sniffling Cara down the hallway to her room. "Rest a while. Are you in any need? Do you wish to talk with me?"

She wagged her head and flopped onto her belly. "I'm fine."

"Aye, then. Bridget shall bring your tea. Blackie, up." Mick shut her door.

The dog lay against Cara and slowly licked her face. His warmth and presence comforted her, and she relaxed. Why did her muscles ache? She had not raised a shovel. Wings did all the galloping. All she did was tell Billy about the fire. She coughed for a moment and closed her eyes. *I still smell like smoke.*

Someone knocked on Cara's door. She opened her eyes, and her room was nearly dark. It was twilight outside. "Cara-mite, Da says to get you for supper. Can I come in?"

"Yes." Cara scooted upright. Blackie blocked Cara's door and turned his gaze to her. "Come."

Bridget swung open the door. "I made your favorite. Pancakes and bacon. Hurry."

In the kitchen, Mick sat in his usual chair, and his friends, Flash and Wolf, were the only guests left. Flash and his brother were no strangers. She had known the Pawnee men all her life and was comfortable with them. Flash's wide grin lit his brown face. He slid his chair back to stand and sent her a nod. "Miss Cara. It is fine we am here?"

"Absolutely. It's good to see you again."

After they said grace over the meal, Mick interrupted them from digging in. "I wish to thank Cara for her efforts, and none are to mention her part again, aye? Unless she should do so herself."

"Thanks, Da."

They ate in typical silence until their plates were empty, and Mick laid his utensils on the table. "So, macushlas, I've a point of discussion as a family. You know I won a substantial sum from Mr. Holloway in a poker game, aye? Well, I've considered what to do with it and wish to donate it to the repairs of the schoolhouse — meaning our Christmas gifts shall be meager at best."

Cara and Bridget recoiled and spoke their objections over each other. It was tough not to react. "I need a new coat. Can't the Holloways pay for it? They're the richest ones around."

Mick considered for a moment. "I know 'tis not the best thing for us, but here's the thing, macushlas. 'Tis best for the townspeople. America may've taken its time to be good to me, nonetheless, it did. I may now give back. In a way, the Holloways shall be the ones to pay for the reconstruction after the fire, shan't they? 'Twas their own money I won. God often has a surprising sense of humor, He has."

The sisters frowned at each other across the table. Cara crossed her arms. *Da trapped us by citing God, gambling and payback in his plan.* What can one say to that? No matter what objections Cara shared, she would sound selfish. As would Bridget. *Plus, Da won that money, and it's not ours.*

Cara shrugged. "It's fine with me. But I must clean myself up. May I be excused?"

Mick grinned. "I'd a feeling I could count on me girls. And Cara, no need to care for the livestock. Flash, Wolf, and I shall take care of that. Do what you must, aye?"

Bridget blew out a breath. "I agree with Cara, and there's no need for you to help me, Sis."

Cara got up from the table and gave Flash, and Wolf a smile. "No wonder you brothers haven't been here for a long while. Look what Da recruited you for? First the barn reinforcements, now my chores, you'd best hide, or he might give away your money next."

***

CHAPTER 8

HER BEST CHRISTMAS GIFT

First one awake and up in the Muldoon's home the following morning after the school fire, Cara tiptoed through the house and prepared herself to exit into the frigid morning. She had not yet heard the rooster crow. A quick glance out the frosty window showed no light on the eastern horizon. "Hey Blackie, we'll be done with our chores early today."

Blackie wagged his tail and waited for her at the front door.

Scampers had not reappeared, and she feared the worst had happened to him, although she could not blame the cats or owls who viewed him as a tasty morsel. Still, her chest twinged. Somehow, his disappearance evoked the loss of Finn and Callum in her mind. She tugged on the bootlaces to test them. "Let's go."

Blackie stepped aside for her to exit first, as a gentleman dog ought.

Cara turned to latch the door, faced back toward the barn, and tripped almost headlong over several packages on the porch. She grasped the porch railing to break her fall. What in the world? Who put those here? There were three brown packages, a stack of notes, two frozen pies, a basket of what smelled like orange cranberry bread, and three jars of something. Cara lifted one jar into her lantern's light. "Cranberry jam."

Blackie sniffed the basket, and she stroked his head. "Back, boy. Sorry, nothing for you. Unless you've got a treat in a wrapped package."

She transferred the items inside the door on the floor for her family to take care of later. What were people thinking, and why? Leaving foodstuffs in the middle of the night where a person could trip over them. It was always anybody else's guess because she never knew how people thought.

Blackie trod down the porch stairs, and she followed him with her steps crunching on the frozen snow and carrying the egg basket and lantern. Its golden glow lit all their footsteps and those of any visitors over the past few days, which marred the snow between home and barn.

"Eager to work, boy?" Her clouded breath hung suspended for a second in front of her, and she patted her scarf back into place over her lips and nose.

In the vast indigo sky, a thin crescent moon shone low above the barn's roof and beyond it, a million bright stars winked at her as though they knew the Almighty's next plan. Another unusually clear December day. Maybe He shall send us a snowy Christmas and Liam with it?

Behind her and the dog, a glow shone from the side of her home. "I bet Bridget is up." Cara swung around to check. Her sister was indeed in the kitchen. "Shall I turn back to get a hot coffee, or wait? We're only ten steps away from it."

Buttercup released her eager lowing at that moment, which convinced Cara's heart. "Whoever doesn't believe in signs is oblivious. Keep going ahead, boy. It was just a temptation."

Cara went about her daily list of chores, bringing joy to her critters, and a sense of daily purpose to her existence. Milk Buttercup, share some with Tricky and Boo, feed Wings and Storm, break up the frozen water in the troughs, throw seed to the chickens, and collect the eggs, feed the skittish sheep, and shovel up the fresh manure. She should return at midday to finish the rest of the cleanup because much of it had frozen to the ground. Besides, her arms ached a little this morning.

Back at the house and while removing her outdoor clothing, Cara appreciated the crackling heat from the wood stoves, and the clunk of iron pans against iron in the kitchen portending breakfast. A good sister would help to put the meal on the table. "Hey, Sis, need some help in there?"

"Please do. You've done your own work, I know, but Da must be away to his crew soon, and I've a terrible mishap with the leftover bread. I wish I knew what to do. I enjoy reading the *Ladies Home Journal* and *Good Housekeeping* when I can get them, yet —"

"We'll do this together, you'll see." Cara entered the warm room with the fresh eggs and milk. On the extra chair, lay the neatly stacked packages, and notes as well. "Morning, Da. Glad you saw those — I nearly broke my neck sprawling over them in the dark."

Mick grinned at her. "None of us be wishing harm to our heroine, aye, Blackie?"

The dog woofed and leaned against Mick's leg for an ear rub.

Cara set the milk pail and eggs on the counter, then snatched the second apron from its wall hook. "I'm no heroine. Are you ready for me?" She stood beside Bridget, who was mittened up and frowning in concentration on her dilemma.

"See that?" Bridget used her elbow to show her sister what baffled her. "The bread is all moldy. Moldy? How did that happen? It's not supposed to, you know. I took great care in following the instructions on how to store it. What shall I do? Da can't go to work hungry —"

"Mount Bridget, didn't you see the cranberry bread that was on the porch?"

"On the porch?"

Cara turned to their father. "Da, you didn't show it to her?"

Mick raised his gaze from the map and the dispatch, probably from his employer. "Was I supposed to? All were gifts for you, by the notes I read. Why show them to Bridget, aye?"

Being this man's daughter explained so much about herself. Obliviousness must be inherited. Cara giggled. She couldn't restrain herself. Glancing at Bridget's confused expression opened the floodgates of hilarity until her side hurt from laughter.

Her sister scowled. "You're laughing in the middle of this disaster? And why do —"

"*Macushla*, Cara, did you injure your head yesterday? Take up a chair and rest for a while."

"I'm fine. I'll explain what made me laugh later." Cara grasped the cranberry bread, careful to set aside the accompanying note, and unwrapped it on the counter. "I'll slice it up, Sis, and you can finish the eggs for Da. There're plenty for all today."

Bridget's brow furrowed, but she finished scrambling the eggs. "I'm eager to know the story, although more eager to get Da on his way. I wonder who baked the bread? If it was that Mrs. Dawson, well we should all think twice about eating it. Quick, Cara-mite, check the note. Do you know I heard from Sheila that Mrs. Dawson nearly poisoned her husband one night at supper when she accidentally put —"

"It's from Mrs. Thompson."

"Well, I'd say that's not much better because she's never liked Auntie O. Do you think she thinks that she's still visiting us?"

"Da's waiting for his meal." Cara placed two thick slices of cranberry bread on a plate and knifed some butter from its tub. "Do you wish for some jam as well, Da?"

Mick folded his map and message. "Nay. Let's say grace and eat."

After breakfast, Mick wiped his mustache, then stood and gently waved the telegram. "Girlies, I've news that Liam and I shall work at a closer distance to each other today. I intend to send him a note by rail and ask if he shall be home with us for Christmas Day. Say a prayer, aye? I must be away."

Cara clattered her fork against her plate. "Truly? Liam may be here?"

Mick kissed her forehead. "We'll see. Don't let your hopes fly away with you. He's quite a far bit of a distance with his crew at the end of the rails. And you know the weather dictates many things."

Bridget clasped her hands. "We'll say an earnest prayer every day. Surely God and the *Chicago, Milwaukee, St. Paul, Railway* will let him come home to us. Could they make the name any longer? Why can't they use initials instead? What if we forget one of those names when we pray? Will God know what we're asking? And another thing, the railroad's got a lot of men who don't need to go home, or have anyone to —"

"Use your worry beads." Mick kissed his middle daughter's cheek. "Pray and see what happens, Bridget. Cara, rest at home today. I'll be home at sunset for supper." He twisted back to his daughters. "Meant to tell you, our town is having a Christmas bazaar in two days to raise funds for the school. What I won from Holloway may not cover the entire expense. Think of something to sell, will you? See you tonight."

A shiny object lay on the floor beside Mick's chair. "Da dropped his compass. Be right back." Cara palmed it, and Blackie rushed out after her.

Her father wasn't yet near the barn, for his limp slowed him down. It pained him more in the cold weather.

"Da! Won't you need your compass?" Cara and the dog strode after him. She had left the house without her outer winter clothing, and the bitter cold air stung her lungs and body. If only she had fur like Blackie, or a hide like Buttercup. If she were an animal, she'd be a newborn squirrel needing its tail as a blanket.

"Aye, me girlie. Now get back inside." He collected the compass from her and tried to hide something poking out of his coat's pocket. A bottle. "Make haste."

No. He's drinking again. Please, not the whiskey. But of course it would be.

Cara plodded quickly to the house with the dog. Flurries whirled around her, and she turned her face up to what had been a clear sky earlier. Tiny frozen dots, more like sleet, hit her face with the increase of wind. She should've told Da to be safe.

Bridget met her at the entryway. "I saw your coat and wondered what you were thinking. Did you catch Da before he left? I was worried that —"

"I did. But Da had a whiskey bottle in his pocket. He's drinking again. Do you think it's because of the cold?" She chewed her lip.

"It's always his aches and pains, you know." Bridget embraced her little sister. "Don't let it bother you too much. He promised it's rare, and we should believe him. Let's focus on praying for him and Liam and thinking up an idea for the fundraiser, alright?" She walked them over to the common room chairs by the heated woodstove. "I've got an idea. Let's make Christmas ornaments to sell. Don't you think it's perfect timing? We can use the boys' old diapers, and I saved some flour sacks for sewing projects. What do you think?"

No worries for Da? How could she not be afraid for him? Yet, she could do nothing about anything. Only God could do miracles. It seemed her family needed many of those right now. Her heart thumped fast and she licked her lips. "I think you should do the sewing, and I should do the measuring and cutting. Remember my bloody fingers from last time? I want them without all those pinpricks and whole for important things, including my chores. But first, we should pray for Christmas miracles for our family."

They recited the *Our Father* together, and the sisters added their burdens for the family, their requests for their father's safety, and desires for Liam and Moira to come home. That would be Cara's own best gift.

A train whistle blew from the direction of the east as it pulled into the town's small station, and Cara went to the front window facing town. She wiped it off with her sleeve. "The sleet stopped. I think the wind blew the storm west."

"The wind controls every storm." Bridget returned to sewing their little brother's blue mittens closed after Cara stuffed them with pieces of rags. "We'll keep these, but there could be fun things we can donate to the Christmas bazaar. Hey, you didn't open your gifts from the townspeople yet. You should check what's inside those packages. There might be a critter in one."

"Open them without Da at home?" She hesitated. Bridget could be right. "Da will see them when he's home for supper, I guess."

Bridget brought her flour-sack stash from the pantry and laid it on the table to show Cara while she ripped open a package. "I think we can make angels out of these. I got some patterns from the *Good Housekeeping* magazine. That was last year's Christmas edition. This is one good reason I keep all those — although Da doesn't like it. One never knows when we'll need them, right? We can dye them with the tea I have in the pantry or keep them all white. Do you have any suggestions?"

"What about little Baby Jesus all wrapped up in blankets? Like we did for Finn and Callum?"

"That's sweet." Bridget's eyes shone with unshed tears. "Sometimes, Cara-mite, I wish you didn't talk about them so much, then again, I'm happy you do." She swiped at a tear trickling down her cheek.

"I'll draw out the angels and Jesus. It's fun to draw again." Cara had stored her pencils and other drawing materials for four years now. Wasn't it time she used her skills again? God surely intended her to create things, but she had not been in the mood since Beth and the boys disappeared. *I'll draw as a sign to God that I've found a little more faith in Him.*

Bridget searched in their father's room for the box Beth had left behind for diapers to cut up for more ornaments, and Cara was nearly finished cutting out the angels, when Blackie scrambled to his feet and woofed.

Someone knocked on their door — Blackie yipped and stood with his paws against it. "I'll answer it, Bridget. Blackie, down."

Cara peered through the frosted window to find out who would visit mid-morning. A hooded young woman in a dark cape sprinkled with snow, red hair poking out from under the hood, turned her face, and — "Moira!" She yanked the door open and squealed.

Moira let her travel bag thud onto the porch as they wrapped each other in a warm embrace, while Blackie darted around their legs in excited loops, and Bridget enveloped them both in an unyielding squeeze of a boa constrictor. They laughed until they could not breathe.

When they broke their embrace, they all fell apart with joyful tears. Six years without a visit. Now this fantastic surprise. A miracle from God. *Thank you for my best Christmas gift.*

Bridget dabbed at her eyes. "I wish we knew you were going to be with us because Auntie O was just here, and we may've urged her to stay longer —"

"I'm sorry. I told Da to keep it a secret in case anything might interfere with the plan. That would be so disappointing, but the church often must be flexible with current events and happenstances. All under God's will, of course. Let me look at you both."

Cara shivered and gathered Moira's travel bag, then led her sisters inside. "We should go inside. We're all together now, so let's get warm. Unbelievable. Isn't it?"

Moira stared up at Bridget and smiled. "You're the tallest of us now, and Cara, I think you'll not grow any further. We're short, medium, and tall, aren't we? A sample of divine womanhood."

The overjoyed sisters took Moira to Bridget's larger room they had shared when Moira was still living at home. They settled Moira while Blackie sniffed her travel bag, probably for clues of where she'd been. Cara patted his back. "If you can figure out the answers to our curious questions over the last six years, boy, let us know."

Moira wasn't dressed in her habit, but her metal crucifix glittered in the winter sunlight through the window. Her long, red wavy hair was now cropped close to her head, and it suited her delicate features. *I'd look like an orangutan if I cut mine like that.*

"The room's unchanged, Bridget, and I didn't expect that. Except now, Cara, you have Liam's old room. How is it not sharing a bed with Bridget any longer? I think it must be close to heavenly."

Bridget startled and scowled at her eldest sister. "Hey. I'm not as restless a sleeper that you always accused me of being, although you're a nun. Why, only the other night —"

"It's true, Moira." Cara laughed. "Are we supposed to call you Sister Elizabeth while you're here? I have a difficult time remembering. You'll always be our sister, Moira."

Moira scanned the room and whispered. "I won't tell anyone if you don't."

Bridget stepped out of the bedroom into the hallway. "Come see what we've been making for the Christmas bazaar. You can help us now that you're here. We've today and tomorrow to finish. I wonder what others are —"

"Keep walking, Mount Bridget, or we'll never escape the hall until Christmas morning with all your chatter." Cara took her older sisters' hands, and hooked together like train cars, they entered to the kitchen to inspect the completed Christmas bazaar ornaments. Others in various stages of creation were spread out with the scissors, needles, and threads.

Moira selected a Baby Jesus. "I wish to take this one with me. May I?" She nestled the little stuffed Jesus in her palm. "How much are you charging for them?"

Cara and Bridget exchanged glances. "We don't know yet, do we, Bridget? But you should take it. Your payment can be through your prayers for the school and for Liam to come home as well."

Bridget fluttered her fingers. "I agree. Your prayers should be worth quite a lot. Do you know, Moira, it once took months of prayer to get justice for that creepy Clyde Harlow? I can tell you —"

"Months? That's a short time in God's eternity." Moira tucked Baby Jesus into her skirt pocket. "Nevertheless, you can count on my prayers. So, tell me all your news. But shall I get the kettle perking first?"

"You're the guest." Bridget filled the silver kettle with water and set it on the stove. "Cara-mite has an admirer. Billy Horan. He liked her before the fire, but now he's well and truly smitten with her. You should see the gift he left on the porch last —"

"Wait. What fire?" Moira widened her eyes to enormous blue ponds.

Cara cupped her own face. Somehow, she must stop the town's appreciation gifts madness, and she did not know how she felt about Billy's gift of perfumed sachets. *Does he think I'm smelly?*

***

CHAPTER 9

HER CHRISTMAS EPIPHANIES

The three Muldoon sisters spent their morning finishing up the twenty-five ornaments of Baby Jesus, singing angels, and stars. Cara added the last touch with her lead pencil on an angel's face and open mouth. "I think I'll dab on some cranberry juice for rosy cheeks. But I'm no Rosie O'Neill."

"The Kewpie doll creator? I've seen those. Most adorable little faces." Moira leaned in closer to Cara. "The cheeks would be a lovely touch. Let me get the jar of the jam you told me about."

Bridget pointed at the pantry. "In there. We can do the same on the Baby Jesus ornaments. How do you want to decorate the stars, Cara-mite? Gold paint would be beautiful if we had some. Can you put smiling faces on them as well? You know, I always wondered if they do smile because God made them so bright? It must be a lovely view from up there. And quiet. If I was a scientist, I'd certainly find out how —"

"How quiet they are, Mount Bridget? Stars aren't people."

"Well, neither are animals, but you treat them like they are."

Moira sat on her chair again and handed Cara the jam. "You're still bickering, I see. I expected it however — I can tell you I don't miss that at all. So, let's change the subject. I know about the fire, the church bazaar tomorrow, and Billy Horan, but is there anything else of interest?"

Bridget spoke around the needle protruding from her lips. "There's the Christmas dance in two days." She slid a quick glance at Cara, who dropped the angel she had added blush upon.

Cara fought again with her swirling emotions on whether to attend. She wished to avoid it, but how could she justify not attending the best event of the year? "I think Bridget should go without me. I'd rather stay home with you, Moira."

Bridget yanked the needle from her lips. "No, you're not. You're the town's heroine, and everyone will want to see you. Can you imagine their terrible disappointment they would —"

"Heroine? I'm not. That's not me. I only did what anyone else would do if they saw a building on fire. Why —"

"Cara, lower your voice." Moira stroked her long braid. "Take a deep breath. For some reason we may never know, you were the one who saw it. Allow the people to be grateful. Not everyone is, you know. It's good for them to feel it and not take their welfare for granted. Are there any clues on how the blaze began?"

Cara shrugged. "Da may know. The men might've talked about it. No one has told me."

"I've heard nothing as well. But I'm in the house most days. I suspect it's a Harlow person. That family has some wicked people in it." Bridget didn't glance up from the Baby Jesus' body she sewed shut and snipped off the knotted thread.

"Clyde Harlow is still in jail for being a creep." Cara inspected a star.

"What about his brother, Harry? I heard he got released a while ago because he's not as depraved. Why would they ever let anyone out of jail that's like him? Do you know Mary Calhoun? Well she said one time when she was home alone, she saw him peeking in at her from outside —"

"Bridget." Moira groaned. "I asked if there were any clues, not accusations."

Goosebumps spread up Cara's arms. Could it really be Harry?

Where is he now? "Sally O'Reilly is stopping by soon to pick up our ornaments to sell. They're all ready, right?"

Bridget sorted and stacked the ornaments in a basket. "Just about. Glad it's not snowing. These should stay dry as long as the clouds stay away. Did you know that damp cotton —"

"Back to the dance." Moira massaged her neck. "Where will it be, and who's invited?"

Cara crossed her arms and stared at the window. This was a subject she didn't wish to discuss or address. That's right. No dress. She cut her glance to Bridget. "You can tell her about it. I don't have a party dress to wear."

"You can wear one of mine." Bridget giggled.

"I'd need to grow a foot in eight hours, right? Is there anything in the pantry for that?" There was no way they could find any dress to fit her from taller and bigger Mount Bridget's closet.

"Maybe there's something of Beth's in that chest she left behind. We can look. Da's not home." Bridget laid the Baby Jesus down on the pile of others. "I'm done with sewing, so I can start on altering. This'll be so fun seeing Cara in a feminine dress." She gave a brief hop. "No one will recognize her, do you think? We could dip her hair in coffee and make it dark brown. Oh, my goodness! Then we can dab some cranberry jam on her cheeks and lips, so she'd be —"

"A doll?" Cara jumped out of her chair, while Moira's jaw hung open. Cara stared in horror at Bridget. "You'd do that to me? What are you thinking?"

Bridget laughed. "I'm teasing you, silly. You're our baby sister, but I know you wouldn't allow us to do that. However, you do need a gown of some sort. I'll see what might be in Beth's trunk." She strode down the hall.

"Our Bridget does allow her imagination to run off with her, you know, Cara." Moira covered Cara's shaky hand with her strong one. "Sit with me. Tell me what you object to about the dance. Nevertheless, I want you to go and to leave me some time alone with our father."

When Moira raised one brow accompanied by that tone of voice, Cara knew her arguments would not prevail.

Cara lowered her gaze to her lap and folded her arms. "Several reasons. The dance is at Josie Holloway's home. I don't fit into a fancy setting. It gives me nightmares to think about it."

"Ah, the Holloway's. And?"

"I truly don't have a gown to wear. They'll laugh at me because I'll look like a scarecrow or a hobo from the rails. I am a railway man's daughter, a farm girl, and not a fancy girl. So, why would I wish to be with those people?" Cara rubbed away tears, then straightened herself. "I'd be brave if you went with me. Will you?"

Moira rose and encircled Cara with her arms. Her little sister leaned back against her. "No, *macushla*, I want time alone with Da. Next, I know you're uncomfortable, but people can be that for shy ones. Christmas is for all of us, and you ought to celebrate with the townspeople's children of your age. You'll one day be out among them, and you must have the awkward experiences along with the blessed to mature into adulthood." She kissed Cara's cheek.

Bridget scurried back. "Look what I found! Bridget's yellow dress. It'll suit you, Cara-mite." She held it against herself, then Cara. Surprisingly, it was not overly big.

"With minor alterations, it should fit. Thank heavens Beth was petite like you. Did you see it against me? More like a shirt. It barely hit my knees. I'd cause a scandal if I —"

"You certainly would." Moira sat beside Cara. "What do you think? Will it do for a farmer's or railway man's daughter?"

Cara fingered the cotton dress. The fabric wasn't lavish, so it was more to her liking. "I suppose God wants me to go because He miraculously provided a Christmas dress I'd wear. I can't argue with Him or Moira." She eyed her older sisters towering over her. "How much effort will it need to become acceptable to those snooty Holloways? Will it take until Christmas 1910?"

Bridget snorted. "No. More like until when you marry a president."
***

The night of the dance on the twenty-third, the weather hung around in a threatening manner. Gloomy all day, with a chill wind — more typical for December.

Cara peered out of her bedroom window after she dressed in time to view Mick pulling up the sleigh with Wings in the encroaching twilight. *Those pretentious Holloways. Expecting us all to leave our cozy homes at night just for them to show off their wealth.*

Blackie slid through the doorway and sniffed her newly adorned skirts. No fooling him. *He smells our Bridget.*

She shook out the full folds of fabric, straightened the lace Bridget had added to its collar, and gave herself a peek in the small mirror above her wash basin. *What could she do to tame her frizzy hair? Only a braid could flatten it.* She returned her silver brush to her bureau and opened Scamper's drawer. Empty. *Of course.*

Her sisters entered together, and Bridget clapped. "Oh, Cara, how you've changed — oh no. You can't leave your hair down. It's an evening event." Bridget turned to Moira.

"You're asking me — a nun, for I go to evening socials three times a week."

Bridget circled Cara, and lifted handfuls of her curly, frizzy hair, twisted it, mumbled at it, and grimaced into Cara's reflection. "What can we do about this?"

Cara slapped her sister's hand away. "Stay back. I don't care. I'll braid it as usual." She deftly wove her long red hair, then turned her head back and forth. "There. I look like myself."

Bridget flopped backwards on Cara's bed, then quickly sat up. "Heavens. I'll wrinkle my gown. I can't go if —"

"Fine by me."

Moira took ahold of Cara's long braid and wound it into a bun. "Bridget, get the hairpins."

It agonized Cara for her sisters to fuss over her and poke her head with sharp objects. "Ow! Are you done torturing me?" She swung away from their busy hands. "I'm staying home in my room with Blackie, so Moira can visit with Da."

Moira stroked Cara's arm. "Check your reflection. You look like a grownup version of yourself. Nothing too drastic. Perfectly presentable."

Her reflection showed the same Cara. She attempted to see inspect her profile. "Not terrible, I suppose."

Bridget gathered her blue skirts. "You'll be a smash at the dance. It's getting late. Come on. It would be terrible if we made it this far only to lose our way in the dark."

When Cara and her sisters entered the common room where their father sat in his armchair by the woodstove, he stood. "At last. Relieved to see you, I am. The light is — Cara, I've seen that dress somewhere — ah, 'twas Beth's, aye?" He circled his two daughters with tears glimmering in his eyes. "Gone are the little *macushlas* I once had who'd sit upon me lap and play. These arms miss holding you, nevertheless, these eyes enjoy beholding you. May this night be magical." He kissed each daughter on their moist cheeks and swiped his fingertips against his own. "We must be away."

The Muldoon family slid smoothly on their excursion hitched securely to capable Wings, and toward the faint glow on the horizon.

Cara adjusted her wool blanket up higher. "At least in the dark we can't miss where they live. It's like a second sun arising. I hope Moira lit all the lamps and put them in our window for beacons on our return, Da."

"Aye, for your eldest sister's a good and thoughtful housekeeper. She knows what to do for safety's sake."

"Unlike me, your middle daughter, Da? You're teasing me." Bridget gripped the seat's back. "Let's sing some Christmas carols. How about —"

"Let's not. You'll need to protect your voices for the dance, aye? 'Twill be boisterous in the home with music and the crowd. We're not on a very long jaunt as well."

Dearest Da. Thank you. Cara clutched the blanket in her fists and breathed in deep and back out again. If she were an eagle, she'd take flight toward home. No such luck. Moira said this experience will help me mature from a child. I like childhood better.

The Holloway's two-story manor increasingly glowered against the bottom of the heavy clouds for the past mile as they approached. Was it foreboding or welcoming? Were her own emotions affecting her perception or was it a warning sign? Cara shuddered.

Bridget squealed. "Isn't it just beautiful? I'm so happy we're invited inside. I've always wondered how they live and in what sorts of luxury. I mean, they have money and lots of it, unlike anyone else we know. Do your best to be polite, Cara, although you detest Josie. We cannot afford to offend her mother. Have you heard the town's stories about her? Well, I have, and I can tell you that—"

"*Macushla*, me curious Bridget. Answer me this — how difficult is it for the poor to offend the rich?"

"Oh, Da. You've made your point. We're almost there. Look at their windows. Each has a wreath with ribbons, and I see people dancing already. Hurry, Da, the music has begun."

Cara stared at the holiday celebration while piano, flute, and fiddle notes swirled around her head. Did she even recall any dance steps? *An immediate hiding place is my goal. If I were Scampers, I'd look for the pantry.* But the kitchen is sure to be staffed to overflowing. *Where can I hide?*

Mick pulled Wings and the sleigh exactly to the front entry decorated with garlands and red bows wound around the posts. The door opened, spilling warm golden light into the dark blue frigid air. He climbed down and escorted his two daughters up the steps to the awaiting Mr. Holloway himself.

"Good evening, Muldoon and family. Welcome to our home. I've been watching for your arrival, Cara. You're the heroine of the hour and everyone wishes to speak with you. Muldoon, you've raised a fantastic young woman." He extended his hand to her father.

Just as I thought, they'll be fawning, and asking a thousand unanswerable questions. Hiding is imperative because Da won't take me home.

"Mr. Holloway, we're grateful to attend your Christmas celebration tonight." Bridget curtsied. "Has the dance begun? We've heard the music for a while now." She craned her neck to peek through the nearest window.

"Oh, my, my, yes." He pushed to door open wider, and the party sounds increased three-fold. "Pardon my lengthy greeting. Go to the parlor on the left to leave your wraps with the housekeeper, and the dance hall is down on your right. You'll find the rest of the help is busy serving Christmas treats you're sure to enjoy, young ladies. Muldoon, I've men to attend to your horse. Come inside for a game of cards with the fathers, and I've a few questions about your new crew. Must not speak of business where Mrs. Holloway might hear that I'm talking business and create quite an uproar."

May I stay with Da until it's over? Where's the cardroom? Cara scanned her father's face and hoped she kept those thoughts to herself.

Bridget grasped Cara's arm. Probably to keep her from bolting out the still open doorway. "The party is underway without us. It's so thrilling. I don't want to miss a thing." She tugged Cara to the parlor where stacks of outerwear were laid on a long rectangular tabletop or over chairs. The silent housekeeper had separated men's from women's clothing. She nodded and gave them a slight smile with her curtsy.

The sisters exited the parlor to head to the dance hall where Bridget immediately met Mary Calhoun. They linked arms and chattered about someone or something or other.

Cara scooted toward the stairs, away from the dance hall. Perfect timing to hide. She peered back toward the parlor and entryway. No one was present to catch her. Which room? Which hallway? Upstairs? Do they creak?

Voices approached. Cara yanked open the small door under the stairway and slipped inside to close it. Pitch dark except for the thin strip of light between the door and the floor. This spot won't do. Her tummy growled. She had no supper. Where's the dining room? Surely there were some delicacies awaiting.

A few minutes passed, and Cara carefully unlatched the small door. She peeked around it. Further past the dance hall, light shone through a wide doorway. She tiptoed with stealth to it and slithered into the empty room. A long sideboard laden with serving dishes sat on the left side of the large dining room, with the ornate table and chairs in the center. A beautiful centerpiece of candles, greenery, and poinsettias adorned the white satin tablecloth beneath a crystal chandelier. No one guarded the room, so Cara helped herself to the platters and bowls of Christmas candy. The candy cane hoard reignited her consternation with Josie, however, there were also sugary red, white, and green Christmas Ribbons, white Divinity, and something new — Hershey's milk chocolates. She unwrapped one and popped it into her mouth. Meltingly smooth, sweet —

"Well, now Miss Cara Muldoon. You must have a powerful sweet tooth to break from social manners. Or perhaps you don't know what they are."

Cara nearly choked on the chocolate, gulped what did not stick to her tongue, and slowly twisted around. Josie, with her arm looped through Billy's. No surprise. Her hot face betrayed her attempt to appear unnerved in the face of Josie's bullying.

"Don't you agree, Billy?" Josie snickered.

He slowly removed Josie's arm. "Pardon me, Miss Holloway, but I'll join her and try your bounty of Christmas candy. Never had the chocolates. Are they as good as rumored?" Billy smiled at Cara.

She nodded, and he handed her another one.

"Josephine Anne Holloway, what are you doing deserting your guests? People are inquiring on your whereabouts. Come with me this instant." Mrs. Holloway extended her hand, and her scowl was enough to make Cara want to obey her.

Josie stomped her foot. "But Mother, I was with Billy and we —"

"Now." Mrs. Holloway sniffed at Billy and Cara, grabbed Josie's arm and led her away.

Billy turned back to the array of sweets and gave Cara a side glance. "Never been so relieved in my life. Have you ever tried to have a full conversation with that Josie girl? She can't talk about horses because she doesn't like them. She can't talk about anything but clothes and rich people. Who's interested in that stuff?" He sucked on a Christmas Ribbon and raised his brow.

"Not I. I don't envy you being stuck with her."

Billy switched the hard candy to one side of his mouth. "For nearly an hour. Glad to see you're here. Was afraid you'd avoid it because of the way the town worships you. Did you eat enough to wait for supper? Don't these people know we eat early to get up early?"

"I guess they don't know." Cara fumbled with her wrappers. Now what? Should she tell him her plan? She scanned the buffet tabletop for a bowl to toss the foil.

"Take another piece. Shall we find a place to sit? Unless you'd rather dance. Do you?"

He stood closer than she had experienced. His arm brushed hers. Why was her mouth so dry? "I would like a drink first. Is there a punch?"

Billy hustled over to a large, crystal bowl that sparkled beneath the chandelier's light. "Here. I'll carry these for us. What about the stairway? People won't look up and see us there."

"Sure." Cara flushed from her neck to her cheeks. *Silly girl.* This doesn't mean anything.

Do I want it to mean something? She followed Billy, and no one interrupted them. They sat with their drinks on the top step before the landing. The music carried upward, but carols were fun.

Billy broke into her introspection with his deep voice. "If I know you well, you'd rather be home with your critters, and away from all the questions about the fire, right?"

I shouldn't be nervous. It's only Billy. "Exactly. Plus you never got credit for helping. Why should I be the only one?"

He softly bumped her shoulder. "You can handle it. So, how are Wings and Storm? We haven't seen you at the stables for several days."

"They're fine. My sister, Moira is in town. You know her from school. She's a nun."

Billy eyed her. His brow furrowed. "I do know her. But you're not thinking of following her example, are you? It's noble and all, but I hope —"

"No — I, uh." Her sister strolled past the staircase. Cara jumped up and splashed her punch down her skirts. "Wait for me, Bridget. Bye, Billy."

When Bridget spied the punch dripping down Cara's dress, she gasped. "You ruined your skirt! Quick, we'll find you a maid to help clean it up. I was looking for you. Everyone wants to speak with you. What've you been doing?" She turned her gaze upward. Why were you — oh, I see. Sneaky girl. Josie will have absolute fits if —"

Josie scowled as the sisters passed her in the hallway. *This should ruin my school life and this already horrid party until next Christmas.*

"Don't worry about her, Cara. After we find someone to help get that punch out of your dress, meet me back at the dance."

Where's that door under the staircase?

***

CHAPTER 10

CARA'S PERFECT CHRISTMAS

*N*oisy Mister Rooster had a death wish. Cara fought to awaken to his early morning call from troubled dreams of being in a strange church with Moira, who insisted she join her and become a nun. She ran blindly down a maze of hallways. The entire time, someone chased her.

Blackie scratched at her door. She sat up and rubbed her face. The aroma of bacon and coffee reached her room. Home was cozier with both sisters here. We need Liam.

Cara gathered up her warm quilt and turned her doorknob. Blackie rushed in, and over to the bureau. He sniffed at Scamper's old drawer. "It couldn't be." She bent over, nudged Blackie away, and gently slid the drawer open. Scampers nibbled on tiny crumbs of cranberry bread. That'll upset Bridget. "Blackie. Sit, sweet boy, and thanks for finding Scampers. I didn't want him to be alone." She shut the drawer. Time for her Christmas mouse later.

The dog whined, yet followed her out. "You showed me, so I know, and now we must work." Cara blinked against the lamplight in the kitchen, and Moira brought her a cup of coffee with a kiss on the cheek.

"I'm eager to hear about the dance. Bridget seems to be sleeping in this morning. I'll try to make her wait to tell me anything."

Cara yawned. "There's not much to tell, but I only want to answer questions once. Where's Da?"

"He's in the barn with Storm. It wouldn't surprise me if he's doing some of your chores. He was proud of you for attending that dance. He knows it was difficult for you. But you did it."

"Reluctantly. I'm unsure why it matters, but I'm sure you'll tell me after breakfast." Blackie eyed Cara from the kitchen doorway, and she followed him to the entry bench to don her winter work clothes.

Once Cara and the dog arrived at the barn, she sipped the coffee to warm up and wake up. Tricky and Boo meowed their greetings and rubbed themselves against her legs. Her father had fed the chickens, and the sheep yet was nowhere around. Thunderstorm chomped his grain inside his stall and stared at her as though she knew where her father was. "Blackie, find Da."

The dog sniffed the dirt and hay and wound a path over to Wings' stall. He sat and glued his gaze to her. "Da's in there, Blackie?"

He woofed.

Wings nickered, and Cara peered over the edge of his stall. "There he is. Blackie, you're clever."

Mick reclined against the far wall of the horse stall — his head lolled to one side. He snored. "Otherwise I would've screamed like a girl." Cara entered Wings' space and pressed her shoulder against him, so she could squeeze past to her father. She shook Mick's shoulder, then spied the whiskey bottle beside his leg. For an alarming moment, her heart thumped inside her chest and landed in her boots. Not the whiskey. Hadn't he been doing well for so long?

Mick's eyelids fluttered open. He seemed disoriented until his gaze landed on Cara. Then he dug around for the bottle and squinted up at her. "I know you're disappointed in me, *macushla*, nevertheless, me pain's been excruciating. It'll be less so in the Spring, aye?"

Wind slammed against the wall, adding more chill to the interior. Cara extended her hands, and her long braid slid over one arm. Although his drinking saddened her, hadn't it been a lifelong challenge for him? She rarely smelled the drink on him anymore. He tries. "Aye, Da. You must get through the winter. Moira has a hot meal for you."

Mick accepted her help to stand. "Are your chores done? Shall you return with me?" They ambled together to the closed double doors, where the wind whistled through the crack.

"Soon, Da. Go inside where it's warm, and I'll be along. The cold sorely increases your aches and pains." Her throat clogged with unshed tears.

Mick kissed her forehead. Only a faint whiff of alcohol accompanied it. He limped out the doors and headed uphill to Moira, Bridget, and the warm kitchen.

With her chores finished, Cara hesitated to return to the house. She was hungry, yet unsure of how to mask her emotions. *Da never neglects us. He doesn't hurt us. His problem is functioning without pain.* "God, please keep him safe and help him continue working to provide for us. That's all he cares about. Amen."

The sheepdog stood beside her, on alert, awaiting her decision. "Let's go in." She reopened the barn doors to a blast of wind, bringing the scent of bacon and coffee in their direction. She breathed in deeply. Her mouth watered. "Someone only invented those to entice the wayward family member's home, don't you think, Blackie? I wish with all my heart that Liam could be here with us."

Blackie wagged his tail at the mention of Liam's name.

Bundled up and face covered, Cara hurried home with the devoted dog. Her only plans now were filling her empty tummy and warming up. Plus, maybe a way to avoid Moira's questions. She stomped her boots on the porch, then entered their home.

Bridget and Moira spoke with their father while he sipped his milk. "But Da, I'm telling you I'm sure Harry Harlow was at the dance and —"

"That man's been in jail for the better part of six years." Mick stood and handed his plate and cup to Moira. He faced Bridget and ran his hand over his wavy auburn hair.

"Yes, I know. But — oh, Cara. You were there. Didn't you see Harry?"

Cara sat in her chair. "I didn't dance. You know where, uh, who I — I didn't —"

"For heaven's sake, I get it. Well, mark my words. Harry has aged, but he's loose, and he started that school fire. Probably to get even with the town for putting him in jail. He's —"

"Creepy? Disgusting? But that doesn't mean he'd burn a building. Can I have my eggs and bacon, please?"

Mick strode to the entry. "'Tis not that I don't believe you, macushla, so I'll ask the crew if they've heard anything. Terrible business, this fire and possibly Harlow. See you at supper, girlies. I wish you a 'Happy Christmas' Eve, aye?"

The sisters chimed the Irish festive expression to him in return. After Mick departed for work, they cleared up the breakfast dishes.

Bridget dried her hands on the towel, hung it on its peg, and tied her red and white striped apron around her waist. "Well, shall we do some baking for tonight, and surprise Da? We can have a pleasant chat while we do it, and maybe I can finish up Finn and Callum's little clothes."

"What do you mean, Mount Bridget? Their clothes for what?" Cara fingered a baby gown Beth had left behind and Bridget found in the chest. Bridget had loaded it into her mending basket. "It's stained and has a few holes. We can't give it to the poor in that condition."

Bridget's brow furrowed. "He existed. Stains mean he was hungry. Beth fed him, or we fed him, because this stain looks like when he ate peas and spit them out. Remember his expression? He couldn't believe we'd stick something repulsive in his mouth, and he was supposed to swallow it." She giggled. "The holes mean life with us was real. We can look at these, a gown, or a shirt, and remember with fondness the happy, loving, and inquisitive tiny brothers who once lived with us and loved us."

Tears swam in Cara's vision, and she blinked them away. "But what's your idea?"

Moira reached around Cara and cuddled the infant gown against her chest. "When you were out with the livestock, we spoke of making these into pillows for ourselves. A tribute to their precious existence and belonging to our family. The 'little boyos,' Da called them."

"I like that, but I'd much rather love them to be back. Wouldn't you?"

Moira wrapped one of her arms around Cara's shoulder. "Absolutely. Until they return to us, we can soothe our broken hearts with these."

The sisters stood together in silence for a moment, gathered around the empty, limp clothes which once covered so much enthusiasm for life. They wiped each other's tears.

Cara tipped her head against Moira's shoulder. "One never knows what to expect from life, or what it might throw our way — I surely didn't guess they'd disappear or stay away this long."

With Moira and Bridget sewing the openings shut to keep the rags Cara had stuffed inside, they all finished within an hour. Finn's short pants and a long sleeve shirt emphasized how small he was at two-years-old. Callum's long stained infant gown filled with the rags resembled a chubby, white two-legged beetle with the stuffed arms poking out.

Cara laughed. "Callum's gown is a chubby beetle. Do we have one of his bonnets?"

Bridget giggled. "You're right. Give me a moment to dig in the basket because I think there's something in the pile. Aren't you glad Beth didn't take everything she —"

"Except for our baby brothers, you mean?"

Moira handed the puffy infant gown to Cara. "Resentment is unhelpful, sister. It gives you no positive strength. In fact, it builds bitterness, and bitterness is self-poison. It makes people cruel. Hold fast any hope in your heart and mind instead because it's one of the greatest strengths and bridges between now and later."

Cara flushed. Her comment twinged her conscience. Unhelpful. She would aim for hope. It was the Christmas season after all, and she could focus on Baby Jesus in the manger — the One Who was hope itself.

Bridget laid one of Finn's shirts in front of Cara. "Here's the last one for you to stuff. I'll put it with their toys when you're finished. Don't you think that would be cheerful? It would be like they're here with us this Christmas, and do you know what I heard from Lucy Howard last week at —"

"Splendid idea, Bridget. I'll find a spot." Moira gathered the gown and other boys' items in her arms and carried them into the common room.

"Wait for me." Bridget scrambled out of her chair around the kitchen table. "Where did we put the extra ornaments that we didn't sell at the Christmas bazaar?"

Cara shoved her chair away and observed her older sisters discuss the best place to display their brothers' toys and stuffed clothing. "I'd stitch up Finn's last shirt, but will probably create an unrecognizable blob out of it. Anyone want to make it look alive?"

Bridget raised her hand. "I will in a minute, Cara-mite."

They set up the display of their boys and toys atop their father's desk beneath the window, with a lit lamp framing it all on either end. The draped swag woven with the mercantile red ribbon bows added color. "What do you think?" Moira straightened the wooden horse, the blocks, and the ball rolled away no longer with Finn's stuffed shirt against it. "We shall finish our day with baking some treats, and Da will be home by then. Won't everything delight him?"

Cara hugged Moira. "I've missed your comforting presence with us. Ordering us about. Passing on your wonderful wisdom. God gave it to you and skipped me entirely."

Moira wrinkled her nose. "You've yet time to learn it."

Bridget laughed. "Well, I'll write you a letter when that happens, I assure you." She returned to the kitchen with a skip in her step. "It's turning out to be a lovely Christmas Eve, and I also found the 'Christmas Cookies' recipe in *The Settlement Cookbook* Da gave to me last Christmas. Do you remember I wanted to make those with you this year, Cara? Now I don't have to force you. Our Moira bakes better than I, and she can help. Don't you just love Christmas? All we need is Liam. I wonder whether he can get here. All this snow we've been having might've interfered. Do you think he's safe? I worry all the —"

"Bridget, your speculation is bothersome." Moira handed Callum's white puffy gown to Cara to snuggle and towed her by the hand to the kitchen. "You may not bake, little sister, but you can cut out the shapes and help make the icing. Plus, whoever has the spoon gets to taste it."

"I recall always fighting with Bridget over the spoon."

"And the conflicts continue yet." Moira dug out the flour, sugar, butter, eggs and vanilla from the pantry, while Cara packed up the sewing supplies from the table with Finn's last shirt on the top.

Bridget gathered the baking pans, measuring cup, and rolling pin. "We haven't talked about Cara and the dance yet, Moira."

Cara scowled. That troublemaker.

"Right." Moira measured flour into the metal sifter. "Tell me how it went."

Cara shrugged a shoulder and squeezed Callum's puffy gown. She wiggled it until the arms flopped up and down. "Not much to tell. People. Music and dancing. Candies. About what one would expect at a Christmas dance. I found all the hundreds of candy canes Josie hoarded. No surprise there. I also ate pieces of Hershey's Milk Chocolate. People haven't overrated it. Could've made myself ill with the entire platter."

Bridget cracked eggs into the mixing bowl. "For heaven's sake, Cara-mite. Tell her about how you happened to sit with Billy Horan on the stairway. All by yourselves. I know there's an interesting story there. You looked so snug together."

Heat infused Cara's face, and she fiddled with Callum's gown. "Nothing happened. Neither of us didn't wish to dance, and he hid from Josie and her mother. Mrs. Holloway snatched Josie away when she found them with me at the candy dishes —"

"Wait. What?" Bridget and Moira paused with their hands in the dough.

Cara grinned and flicked the air. "Billy didn't mind, but you should've seen Josie's face. I can tell you I wish to never return to school. She already detests me. I can't imagine how she'll feel about me now. Spoiled Persian cat."

Moira returned to rolling out dough on the floured board. "You saw envy and jealousy at work. They're powerful and destructive emotions. You might see them often in the future, especially in other women. Beware of it. You can't change people or help them. Although mothers can tackle those when they identify those bents in their young children."

Bridget broke off pieces of dough and rolled them in her sugared palms. "Jealous women are dangerous. Did you hear the story of that wife in Bedford who set her cheating husband —"

"That's enough, sister. It's Christmas Eve, and we should change the subject." Moira set flattened dough onto the oiled pans. "I know you're fifteen, nearly sixteen, Cara, but are you interested in Billy? How old is he?"

Cara fondled the ties on the stuffed infant gown. "I like him. He's seventeen, almost eighteen like Bridget will be. But after what I did, he might not like me. I think I injured his feelings."

Bridget yelped. "My heavens, what did you do to him?"

"He was asking me something, then I saw you go by, and I left him without hearing it all."

Bridget and Moira exchanged confused glances. Bridget narrowed her eyes. "You can fix it when you get the chance. Don't worry, Cara-mite you'll —"

Blackie woofed, scrambled out from under Cara's chair, and then someone knocked on the front door.

Moira wiped her hands on her apron and headed to answer it. "Hello, I remember you. Our father will be home shortly. Oh, sure. Come in. I'll get her."

Cara's heart thumped. Her? That means me or Bridget.

Bridget quickly washed her hands at the sink and dried them, then stood by Cara.

Billy Horan entered the kitchen with his hat brim rolled in one hand, flattened dark hair, and a full, crunchy brown bag in his other hand. He slid his gaze around the room.

Cara flushed from her chest to her cheeks. Oh dear.

He smiled at her. At least he's smiling. "Miss Cara Muldoon, I brought you a bag of candy canes from Josie. She said she owes them to you, and her mother wouldn't allow her to give them to you herself last night. Mrs. Holloway doesn't care for you. Who does she care for? Anyway, will you accept them with her apology, and a Merry Christmas Eve?" He extended the bag.

"What for?" Josie owed her many apologies. Cara laid the puffy gown down and grasped the unexpected gift bag. "Thank you for bringing it." Why would Josie give me this?

"She wishes to be friends. That's what she said." Billy tipped his head toward the entry. "Also, when I arrived, your da spied me from the barn. I planned to leave these on the porch and hurry home, you see, but he instructed me to tell you all that you're to stay in the kitchen and close your eyes." He blushed. "That's all I'm allowed to say. From your Da. That's what he wants."

The sisters frowned at each other, then at Billy. Moira nodded. "You can tell him we agreed."

He swished his hat in front of himself. "I'm told to stay here with you all, make sure you close your eyes, and wait with you. That's what he said."

Cara, Bridget and Moira raised their brows, clasped hands and turned around toward the kitchen window. Snow flurries tumbled past, highlighted by the room's light against the backdrop of blue. What could Da be doing out there? Cara wanted to peek, but the window faced away from the barn.

Blackie left Cara, and another knock sounded on the door. Billy spoke to Mick in tones too low to understand the words.

Bridget whispered. "Can you hear what they're saying? I'm about to burst my brains listening and guessing what's happening."

Moira shushed Bridget and squeezed Cara's hand, and Cara squeezed back.

Blackie whined and yipped, then his claws tapped nearer to Cara on the floorboards. By the pattern of his paws hitting the floor, he jumped up and down.

"Surprise, girls. Happy Christmas!" Liam announced. Chaos ensued with hugs, and cries of holiday greetings, kisses on everyone's cheeks, and their father beamed and grinned as wide as his thick mustache allowed.

Bridget untied her apron and tossed it onto the counter. "Now this all makes some sense, Da. Your request was the strangest thing — well, maybe not as strange as the time you —"

"Not now, macushla." Mick waved his hand. "We've got Christmas Eve to attend to."

Liam's Macedonian friend, Ace, stood to the side with Billy. Ace was on Liam's rail crew and had visited their family with him a few times before. His brown skin was more weathered, and his dark eyes sparkled with merriment.

"Glad Liam brought you, Ace. We've got cookies." Cara handed him one.

"Thank you, Miss Muldoon."

Moira held Liam in a lengthy embrace. "What took you so long to arrive? I've been home for days." She turned her face up to his towering height.

Liam removed his cap and ran his fingers through his red wavy hair. "My crewmen had a near riot and almost hanged me for stealing their money. Ace can vouch for that. He saved my life by helping me, and God saved me by answering my prayer. He's got my attention forever. But more about that later." He backed through the doorway. "Come here everyone, I brought gifts."

The Muldoon family and their guests congregated in the common room, where Mick and Liam inspected the holiday tribute to Finn and Callum lit up by the lanterns, and Cara filled the desk by adding the two new stuffed pillows. They caressed the clothing, inspected the toys, and pretended there were no tears in their eyes. Mick's expression gentled, and he murmured to his daughters. "Delightful idea, me *macushlas*."

Liam slid his hands into his pants pockets and cleared his throat.

"I've an important update regarding my search for the boys at the schools. My fellow *Chicago, Milwaukee and St. Paul Railway* foremen have agreed to help me be on the lookout for any information. Although it's been four years, we can persist in the search if we work united in the goal of bringing them home. Don't you think, Moira, uh, Sister Elizabeth?"

Moira grasped his hand. "I agree with you. We shouldn't give up hope. I've friends sifting through church records, and we're checking orphanages. All while we fulfill our duties to the church. Time is limited, but I believe there're plenty of details to find."

Cara's heart and spirit soared with hope and joy, while tears spilled down her cheeks. These magnificent adults were her family, and they had committed to do everything they could to find Finn and Callum out of love. They didn't give up. "Thank God Himself for your perseverance, Liam and Moira." She squeezed them both.

Everyone else expressed their gratitude, asked some questions, and then Liam retrieved his packages. "I'm eager to see your reactions."

Cara sat with her package and opened it with Liam standing over her. "Sis, there's a funny tale to tell you surrounding your gift. Amy, a helpful friend, chose it because I'd no time to shop. Our isolated, tiny supply town has little to offer, but I hope you like it."

After digging through the box and wads of brown paper, she finally reached the object and tugged it out. A red coat. She nearly laughed. Red.

"Do you like it? I told her small, and to match my hair, for yours is the same color — as that's what all our family has. Only a few coats remained in the store, and brown is easy to find."

Cara chuckled with her family. "Liam. We don't have brown hair — we all have red hair. So, she matched our hair. You must be colorblind."

"What? I am not. Am I?" Liam sat on the nearest chair with his mouth open and stroked his jaw. "The wrong color changes what I've told people for the last several years. I must correct what I've said, for I described the boys with brown hair. This will help us find them — I know it will."

Moira, Bridget, and Mick gathered around Liam, and they embraced each other, then Cara joined them. She brushed her hand over her pristine, perfect new red coat draped over her arm. "Then this is the perfect Christmas gift, Liam, and now red is my favorite color."

THE END

EPILOGUE

*D*ear Readers,

Who says that a quiet and remote life can't be exciting? This is Cara, and I can assure you it's never dull. I'm thrilled you'll be reading my oldest brother Liam's book next summer!

Liam was my only brother until our two younger brothers came along. You've read about them in this book, and that they tragically disappeared with their mother, Beth.

In Liam's book, he will tell his side and part in the story, because he was there. Or not quite there. You'll see what I mean. Bridget and I were at school, Da was at work, and Liam was working on our farm.

That's all I'd better say for now, for he tells the story about his search for them much better than I ever can.

P.S. I still have my red coat and Callum's stuffed infant gown.

Cara Muldoon.

AUTHOR'S NOTES

This is bonus material to the <u>Those Resilient Muldoons</u> series. Cara's Christmas story happens during the missing eleven years in Book 1, *Muldoon's Misfortunes*, between Beth's leaving the family in Chapter 24, 1905, and Chapter 25, when Mick's children are young adults in 1916.

This true incident happened in my dad's father's family, although I fictionalized it to fit the facts. No one is alive for me to ask more details about it, and sadly, I didn't ask questions when I had the opportunity because I wasn't an author then.

Book 3 in the series, *Rescuing the Muldoons*, will follow young Liam's life and how he searched for his brothers. I hope you'll enjoy it.

*Bridget's cooking, (research notes from GROK):

In 1909, American Christmas baking was heavily influenced by European immigrant traditions (especially German, Scandinavian, and British), as well as domestic cookbooks like Fannie Merritt Farmer's The Boston Cooking-School Cook Book (revised editions from 1896 onward) and The Settlement Cook Book (first published in 1901 in Milwaukee, drawing from German-Jewish recipes). Cookie baking was a holiday staple, often involving hand-cut shapes, spices for warmth, and simple ingredients like molasses, ginger, and sugar, which were affordable and shelf-stable. Electric ovens were rare (most used wood or gas stoves), so recipes favored drop or rolled doughs that baked quickly.

Based on period recipes, advertisements (e.g., in Ladies' Home Journal or Good Housekeeping magazines), and baking trends documented in historical sources like the Library of Congress's historic American cookbooks, here are some of the most popular Christmas cookies baked in the U.S. at the time. These were often made in advance, stored in tins, and shared at church events, family gatherings, or as gifts: (I used the 'Christmas Cookies' ingredients list).

*Cara sampled these candies at Josie's Christmas dance, (research notes from GROK):

In 1909, American Christmas candy-making was a blend of homemade traditions (often featured in women's magazines like Ladies' Home Journal and Good Housekeeping), European immigrant influences (e.g., German, Scandinavian,, and marzipan molds), and emerging commercial products from companies like Hershey's (milk chocolate bars since 1900) or Brach's (founded 1904, known for caramels).

*Ribbon Candy

• **Why popular**: Hard candies were shelf-stable gifts; peppermint oil (from apothecaries) evoked winter freshness. Ribbon candy (pulled and striped) was a commercial hit from New England factories, but homemade drops mimicked it.

• **Typical recipe style**: Sugar syrup boiled to 300°F, flavored with peppermint, pulled/thinned, and cut into shapes or drops on greased slabs. Food coloring for red/white stripes.

• **Cultural note**: Filled candy dishes at parties; immigrants added anise or lemon. Store-bought from companies like NECCO (wafers since 1847) supplemented home efforts.

*This rather young author remembers Ribbon Candy from my youth, and NECCO wafers were one of my favorites. What ever happened to those?

THOSE RESILIENT MULDOONS SERIES

Immigrants are courageous, resourceful, and resilient to leave their homelands and settle in an unknown land. The Muldoons are no exception. The series follows Mick Muldoon, and his sister from 1860s Ireland to America, and his eldest son born in the new country.

Irish siblings in the 1860s forsake their careworn family. They dare to immigrate from their verdant island full of poverty and despair. Their hopes lay in America's vast freedom and wealth, yet, the irrepressible Muldoon's peculiar secrets might hopelessly doom their fates.

The Perfect Christmas for Cara: A Country Critters and Clues Novella, reveals one of the many Christmas celebrations in the Muldoon's family with Mick's youngest daughter.

Encountering God's unexpected presence is a main thread for the characters in all of author E. V. Sparrow's stories. May you, the reader, be surprised and awed as well.

Muldoon's Misfortunes, Book 1, is a BookFest First Place Historical Fiction award winner.

MULDOON'S Misfortunes

THOSE *Resilient* MULDOONS
BOOK 1

E.V. SPARROW

MADAM MULDOON'S Garden

THOSE Resilient MULDOONS
BOOK 2

E.V. SPARROW

MULDOON'S
Minnesota
Darling

THOSE *Radiant* MULDOONS

A NOVELLA

E.V. SPARROW

BOOK LINKS

Book 1, Muldoon's Misfortunes
Book 2, Madam Muldoon's Garden
Prequel Novella Muldoon's Minnesota Darling

ABOUT THE AUTHOR

Award winning E. V. Sparrow is a short story writer turned novelist and is an emerging author of literary and historical fiction. She wrote a prequel novella to <u>Those Resilient Muldoons</u> series, and this is Sparrow's second novella. She has also written tow full-length novels.

Sparrow's readers encounter God's unexpected presence through her character's escapades. Her own adventures are short stories, involving traveling in over twenty countries. Sparrow lived overseas for a year and hopped a freight train for a weekend.

A highlight for Sparrow is when Guideposts and Bethany House Publishers accepted four of her anthologized stories.

Her father's dad's family immigrated from Ireland, and saved their photos, letters and documents. Some family stories inspired her current 3-book historical fiction series.

In E.V.'s personal and church life, she ministered through prayer, worship, mission teams, and in Divorce Care and Singles. California native transplant to North Carolina, E.V. Sparrow and her husband enjoy family time with their grandchildren and exploring their new state. Sparrow never misses a day without coffee, chocolate, and feeding her birds, squirrels and chipmunks waiting outside her door in Sparrow Woods.

ACKNOWLEDGMENTS

Thank you to my husband, David, who is a 50+ year graphic artist and created this fabulous cover for me! He creates images, and I create worlds. I think I've got him hooked on book covers now.

My daughter, Hannah Hagen, once again was graciously my editor for this novella. I couldn't write as well without her feedback.

We hope this book blesses your socks off as you sit beside a cozy fire and sip a hot drink.

Your gift of reviews are the best way to support your author friends, and celebrate our achievements. The places to leave reviews are: Amazon, Goodreads, and BookBub.

I wish you merry holidays and that you may receive the perfect Christmas for you as well.

Author E. V. Sparrow.

FOLLOW THE AUTHOR

Instagram https://www.instagram.com/erin.sparrow.world/
Facebook Page https://www.facebook.com/sparrowwriter/
LinkedIn https://www.linkedin.com/in/erin-e-v-s-3438918/
Amazon Author https://www.amazon.com/author/evsparrow
Website https://evsparrowworld.wordpress.com
X (Twitter) https://x.com/evSparrow
Newsletter https://mailchi.mp/475597e34cd3/sparrowworld
Pinterest https://www.pinterest.com/evsparrow/
GoodReads https://www.goodreads.com/author/show/29663267.
E_V_Sparrow
BookBub https://www.bookbub.com/profile/1444307620
Reader's Private Group: https://www.facebook.com/groups/
645009377108035

www.ingramcontent.com/pod-product-compliance
Lightning Source LLC
Chambersburg PA
CBHW030640130626
46552CB00002B/941